THE PURPLE SCAR

AIRSHIP 27 PRODUCTIONS

The Purple Scar Volume Two

"All that Glitters is Death" ©2016 Gene Moyers
"Prescription for the Mob" ©2016 Paul Kevin Findley
"Trial by Fire" ©2016 Erik Franklin
"The Deadly Doppleganger!" ©2016 David Noe

Published by Airship 27 Productions
www.airship27.com
www.airship27hangar.com

Interior illustrations ©2016 Marco Santiago
Cover illustration ©2016 Marco Santiago & Shannon Hall

Editor: Ron Fortier
Associate Editor: Fred Adams Jr.
Marketing and Promotions Manager: Michael Vance
Production and design by Rob Davis.

ISBN-10: 0-9977868-8-4
ISBN-13: 978-0-9977868-8-0

Printed in the United States of America

10 9 8 7 6 5 4 3 2 1

VOLUME TWO

TABLE OF CONTENTS

ALL THAT GLITTERS IS DEATH

BY GENE MOYERS

Dr. Miles Murdock sighed as he eased his trim six foot frame into the swivel chair behind his desk. He glanced at his wrist watch, it was just after 5:00 p.m. and it had been a long day. Even now Dale, his trusted nurse assistant and fiancé, would be locking up out front. He had spent most the day standing on his feet examining and helping what seemed like an endless parade of patients at his Down Street clinic. The day had been productive and thinking about the number of needy people he had helped that day made his weariness bearable. Wishing he had a cup of coffee, he brushed his hand through his curly black hair before unfolding the morning's unread newspaper. A headline on the lower half of the front page immediately caught his eye.

JEWEL THIEVES STILL AT LARGE!

Quickly skimming over the article he realized it did not add much to what he already knew. Two days earlier four hooded, armed men had robbed DeRuyter's Jewelers. They had been violent but no one had been seriously injured. The only updated news the article contained was the value of the stolen merchandise. The robbers had escaped with jewelry now valued at nearly forty thousand dollars. Doc Miles raised an eyebrow over a piercing black eye thinking, *Those crooks had quite a pay day.* He frowned, wondering if Akelton would be undergoing a new wave of violent crime.

Doc was just turning to page two when he heard loud voices from the front of the clinic. He lowered the paper; a moment later a muffled woman's cry came to his ears. In a flash he had dropped the newspaper and was halfway to his office door. Grasping the knob he jerked it open. The small lobby of the clinic was crowded with people. With the exception of Dale, who was crowded back against the reception desk, all of them were brandishing guns and wearing hoods. A thin man in a suit had a pistol pointed at her head. Two more men stood in center of the lobby, one large man carried an automatic in his right hand while the left arm supported another man who had obviously been wounded. The wounded man held a blood stained handkerchief to his left arm with his right hand. Blood had soaked the arm of his dark suit and was even now dripping slowly onto the bright linoleum. A shorter man stood at the glass entry door staring out into the street. One hand held a gun as his other hand turned a key in the lock to secure the door.

Controlling his urge to throw himself at the man threatening Dale, Doc instead asked in a controlled voice, "What's going on here?"

The masked gunman supporting his wounded pal pointed his pistol at Doc and said, "You're a doctor aren't you? We got a patient for you."

Doc stepped forward and spoke quietly. "That man needs a hospital emergency room. I'm a plastic surgeon not a trauma surgeon."

Pointing his pistol at Doc the thug answered glibly, "You're what we've got. So get busy. Or we'll take it out on your pretty nurse." He looked at his companion covering Dale with his gun and nodded.

Surrendering to the inevitable, Doc raised his hands in front of him. "All right bring him this way." He turned and led them down the hall to an examining room. As the wounded man was helped in, Doc pointed to an examining table. "Get him out of that jacket and lay him down there." The wounded man was helped onto the table as Doc began washing his hands. Once he had dried them, he pulled on a pair of thin rubber gloves and moved to the patient. He began cutting open the sleeve of the blood soaked dress shirt. Not looking up from his work he stated firmly, "I'm going to need my nurse in here to assist." He moved to a cabinet and began sorting through small medicine vials. The hooded man on the table nodded and his pal leaned out into the hall and called, "Bring the skirt in here." By the time Dale was pushed through the door Doc had found the vial he wanted and was filling a syringe.

"What's in that thing?" the tall man asked pointing with his gun.

"A local anesthetic for his arm. Dale, I'll need a probe and set of scalpels. Bring plenty of sponges and gauze as well."

Ignoring the tall man's gun and suspicious looks Doc moved confidently to work. He swabbed the wounded man's left shoulder and injected him with the syringe. While the anesthetic began its magic, he turned to help Dale lay out his instruments on a small, moveable table. Satisfied with his instruments he began washing the blood clear of the wounded man's arm. The apparent bullet wound was on his bicep but blood had run all the way to his fingertips. As he washed the man's forehead and hand looking for additional wounds Doc took note of a thin band of un-tanned skin circling the man's ring finger. He didn't linger there but filed his observation away for future reference. Pointing to the wound site he instructed, "Dale, swab around the wound with alcohol." Picking up a long probe he waited for Dale to finish before he began his work. As he gently touched the wound he asked, "Can you feel that?"

The patient replied, "Just barely; it doesn't hurt if that's what you mean."

Doc nodded as he gently worked the probe into the wound. He worked carefully for a few moments before he stepped back and set down the probe. Looking up at the tall gunman he said, "There is a bullet or large fragment still in there. I'm afraid it's got to come out." Before he could reply the patient said weakly through his hood, "Proceed doctor, I trust your judgment."

Taking a deep breath Doc said, "All right, here we go" and reached for a scalpel. Although not a trained trauma surgeon, Doc Murdock was nationally known as a plastic surgeon of great skill. He had helped many victims of tragedy and was highly skilled with a scalpel. Within minutes he had removed the projectile from the wounded criminal's arm. Holding it up to the light in the medical clamp he said, "It looks pretty mangled. I would guess it was a ricochet, that's why it didn't exit cleanly." He dropped the mangled slug into a shallow pan. He took up needle and medical thread and skillfully sewed up the wound. A few more minutes and he had the wound closed and bandaged. He then removed his soiled gloves and he and Dale helped the patient sit up. Doc steadied him while Dale located a white sling to hold his injured arm. As the wounded man slipped off the table he tottered slightly on his feet but was steadied by his still watchful, gun toting companion. As he was leaving the room, the wounded man stopped in the doorway and spoke over his shoulder the voice still muffled by his hood, "Thank you doctor. If you and your pretty nurse will be so good as to remain in this room for five minutes we will trouble you no more."

With a cynical smile Doc inquired, "Where shall I send the bill?" Perhaps there was a muffled chuckle as the door closed behind the two gunmen. Turning to Dale he grasped her arms just above the elbows and looked into her eyes, "Are you all right dear?"

Dale nodded. "A little scared but I'll be fine."

"Good girl." Doc moved quickly to the door and placed his ear against it. He listened but heard nothing. Putting his finger to his lips as he glanced at Dale, he opened the door silently and listened again. Motioning to her to remain, he slipped into the hall. He glanced into the reception area and seeing the door apparently still locked, he moved quickly down the hall and around a couple of corners to the alley door. He opened it slightly and heard a car engine powering away. Jumping out into the alley he just saw the rear of a dark sedan disappearing around the corner of the alley and down the street.

Returning inside, Doc made for his office where he called police headquarters and reported the masked gunmen. He asked for Captain Griffin but was told he was out. While he waited for a radio car to arrive, he was joined by Dale. She sat in an armchair looking slightly pale so Doc poured her a drink to steady her nerves and one for himself as well. Smiling, he sipped and said, "I guess I might have done all right if I'd gone in for trauma work." Dale smiled back weakly at him, "You did fine, darling. It was me who was shaky."

Doc shook his head and inquired, "Did you notice anything unusual about our wounded patient?"

Dale paused, her drink halfway to her mouth, "Other than he was wearing a hooded mask and was bleeding profusely no, nothing out of the ordinary."

Doc looked thoughtful for a moment, "His hands."

"His hands?"

"Yes, his hands. They were soft and his nails were neatly trimmed. Also he had a band of un-tanned skin around his ring finger, as if he normally wore a wedding band but had removed it. I think our victim was no common thug. He also spoke fairly well for a man who makes his way with a gun."

Dale looked thoughtful at this, "You think he was the leader?"

"At least that. I would like to know more about these men and what they're up to." Before Doc could say any more he was interrupted by a ringing bell from the front door. Dale left to check and as Doc suspected it was two uniformed officers. He and Dale were still giving statements to the officers ten minutes later when an unmarked cruiser pulled up out front and Captain Dan Griffin and two detectives jumped out. The square jawed, stocky Griffin strode straight up to Doc, "Headquarters radioed me what happened. Are you and Dale okay?"

"We're fine. No one was hurt; we're just a little shaken."

Griffin's lined face relaxed a little as he nodded, "I can understand that. What happened?"

Doc gave him a thumbnail version of events. When he was finished, Griffin turned to his detectives and quickly gave orders. They immediately began taking photos, dusting for prints and taking blood samples. With things organized, the grey haired captain motioned Doc and Dale toward the back of the clinic. He lowered his voice and adding, "We have to talk." Nodding, Doc led the way to his office. Once there he gave, with Dale adding details, a full account of all that had taken place that evening. When he finished Griffin took over, "When I got your message I was over cleaning up the mess at Danley's jewelry store on 5th. Four hooded men robbed the place just minutes before you had visitors. They got out of the store with a good take but ran into an unlucky beat cop making his rounds. There was a shootout and the cop was wounded before the gunmen got away in a dark sedan. From the blood at the scene we're sure one of the robbers was also wounded. Dale broke in, "How is the officer?" Griffin looked grim as he answered, "He was seriously wounded but the hospital thinks he'll make it." Doc nodded as Griffin continued, "They were seen heading in this direction. I'd be willing to wager they went right down this street saw the clinic sign and stopped for medical help. We are certain this is the same gang that robbed DeRuyter's the day before yesterday."

Doc inquired, "Any idea who they may be?'

"No, as far as we know there's no "smash and grab" gang like this operating locally. We're working all of the usual intelligence sources but these guys look to be new in town."

At this Doc looked thoughtful, "The only one who did any amount of talking was the wounded man and he sounded like a local."

"Anything else you noticed about him?"

A nod, "I think he was the leader. I may have some other things for you soon but first the Purple Scar is going to look into some things tonight."

Griffin stood up. "Right. I'll be going then. Let me know if you 'remember' anything else." Shaking hands with Doc and nodding to Dale he quickly left the office to supervise his detectives.

At this point Doc sent Dale home but waited around for the detectives to finish with their photos and collections. Once all the officials had left, he locked the clinic securely and made his way to his parked roadster. As he motored casually across town, he considered his next moves. Arriving at his Swank Street clinic, he unlocked the door and passed through the well-appointed reception area. Here was where Doctor Murdock catered to his wealthy clients who desired or needed the world class plastic surgery that he was known for. His rates were high but were paid without question for his talent was known far and wide in the medical profession. These rates funded his clinic in the slums and allowed Doc to help many poor and unfortunate clients in need of his services. They also funded Doc Murdock's sub-rosa activities as the menacing Purple Scar. Making his way to his private quarters on the second floor, Doc was greeted by a thin little man with sparse hair. He normally had a somewhat furtive look about him but now smiled widely as Murdock entered his living quarters, "Hey Doc. How was your day?"

"Interesting, Tommy, very interesting. Come along, I have a lot to tell you."

Tommy Pedlar, former second story man and now Doc's aide and confidant, followed Doc past his studio to his private study. Doc seated himself at his desk and Tommy slipped into an armchair while Doc filled him in on all that had happened at the clinic. He listened without comment, although his face darkened when he heard how Doc and Dale had been treated by the hooded gunmen. When Doc had finished Tommy looked expectant, "What do you want me to do?"

"After dinner I want you to go out and hit the usual haunts. Ask about any new guns in from out of town. If you hear of any, try to find out what they're doing. Also ask around about the jewelry thefts. I bet every shady character in town is talking about them. See if anyone knows about hot jewelry hitting the fences in town."

"Right Doc. Report back here later?"

"No. Meet me at the *High Point* bar at eleven. I'll be wearing a gray checked suit. Walk in, look around, and head for the alley behind the bar. Wait for me there."

Tommy nodded and left the room. Soon they both ate a small meal that Tommy had prepared. Once finished, Tommy quietly left down the back stairs. Doc then proceeded to his studio. Going to his concealed safe, he quickly opened it and sorted through the items within. Removing a flexible mask he moved to a mirror and quickly fitted the tight mask over his own features. He smoothed it down and looked at the bland features staring back at him from the mirror. He had chosen one of his favorite pre-made masks to wear. This particular mask showed a face so bland and unremarkable that no one would give it the least interest. Doc then slicked his hair down with some cheap smelling hair oil and smiled at his likeness. He was confident that no one would remember his face five minutes after they met him. Moving on to his bedroom, he changed into a cheaply made grey checked second hand suit that fit him rather loosely.

His last actions before leaving his apartment was to slip his master keys and a pencil flash into his coat pockets and a .38 revolver onto his hip. Finally, he picked up another flexible mask and examined it. This mask, patterned after his slain brothers' scarred features, was a harsh purple in color and had horribly scarred and twisted features. The disguised Doc smiled as the ugly mask disappeared into a hidden pocket of his cheap jacket. Turning out the lights he quickly exited down the back stairs.

Doc started at the *Falcon Club*, a known underworld hang-out. He slunk in, ordered a beer, and nursed it while listening to the gossip. Specifically, he was listening for talk about the recent robberies and any talk of hot jewelry being moved around. There was plenty of speculation about the "new" gang in town but nothing concrete; no names or claims of direct knowledge. Soon he moved on to *Duke's*. It was the same there. Many of the career criminals and other folk on the edge of the criminal world were talking about the recent robberies but no one seemed to have any concrete knowledge. He checked in at several other places but the story was the same: just rumors. He wound up at the *High Point* bar just before eleven p.m.

He didn't have long to wait. Within a few minutes Tommy came in, walked straight to the bar and ordered a beer. He did not acknowledge Doc at all. Doc got up and moved to the rear of the bar. Locating the hallway leading to the restrooms he paused at the men's room door to be sure he was not attracting attention and then slipped down the hallway to what he presumed was the bolted back door. Unlocking it he stepped into the darkened alley and closed the door quietly behind him. Less than five minutes later a dark figure appeared at the mouth of the alley. Doc moved silently toward the figure and whispered, "Tommy."

"It's me Doc."

"What did you find out?"

"I've been to a lot of places. Everybody's talking about the robberies but nobody seems to know anything definite. Nobody's talking about hot rocks, so I think the gang must be sitting on the loot for now."

"Yes, I've heard the same. Well, it's getting late. Knock off for now and head home, and thanks Tommy."

"What about you?"

"I have one stop I want to make first."

Tommy acknowledged and left the alley. Doc gave him a few minutes and then followed. Once in his car, he drove carefully across town. Parking a block away from his destination, he slouched along the last block with his hands shoved deep in his pockets. He ended up across the street from a series of empty store fronts and marginal businesses. They were all closed save for a single storefront with a large sign overhead that proclaimed it to be a pawnshop. As Doc watched, the lights in the store went out. He glanced at his watch; it was just midnight. Leaving his post, he shuffled to the corner, crossed the street and located the wide alley behind the row of shops. He stopped and pulled off his mask and quickly replaced it with the mask of the Purple Scar taken from its hidden pocket. Adjusting it carefully, he pulled his revolver and drifted silently down the alley. At a point he judged approximately behind the pawn shop a sedan was parked. The Purple Scar flashed his pocket light around for perhaps a second to scan his surroundings and then killed the light as he sank down behind a trash can a few yards down from the back door of the pawn shop.

He waited for what seemed like a half hour but was probably only five minutes. Then a lock grated and light from an open doorway flooded the alley and illuminated two figures exiting the building. Rising up silently, the Scar took two quick steps and brought his revolver down on the first man's head. The heavy set man let out a grunt and slumped to the ground. The Scar spun around and raised his revolver at arm's length into the startled face of the second man caught in the beam of his pocket light.

In a raspy voice the Purple Scar grated, "Well, Jimmy McCall. Where are you going to in such a hurry?"

Jimmy "Cash" McCall was a tall, gaunt figure. His suit didn't look as expensive as it was because it hung on his bony frame, his face paled and he whispered, "Purple Scar!" The briefcase he was carrying dropped from one nerveless hand as it joined its brother rising into the air. "Look Scar, I'm clean. I'm not fencing stolen goods anymore."

"Sure Cash, that's why you need a bodyguard," the Purple Scar waved his free hand toward the unconscious figure on the ground. "You may not be fencing high priced items anymore because you know I'm keeping an eye on you. But you're still in the know, that's why I let you live. I need information. Now"

"Wha. . .wha, what do you want to know?"

"I want to know about the new gang in town. I want to know who's moving the hot jewelry they've stolen."

The gaunt fence licked his lips, "Uh, you're not going to believe this, but I don't know, in fact no one knows."

The Purple Scar rasped out, "I find that hard to believe."

"No, it's true. I was just talking to Hard Luck Benny today. We were

"What…do you want to know?"

arguing about who would'a brought in these new guns. Nobody seems to know and nobody's heard anything about the loot."

The Scar was thoughtful for a moment, "Who said these gunmen were from out of town?"

McCall squirmed visibly in the Scar's flashlight beam, "Well, uh, that's the word."

The Purple Scar took a step forward so that his revolver barrel was just inches from McCall's face, "Whose word? Someone must know something."

McCall paled even more. "Uh, I heard that Freddy Larkin said he saw some strange hoods in town a few days ago."

The Scar looked thoughtfully at "Cash" McCall. He'd had a run in with him a few months back. He'd put the fear of God into him at the time and Scar felt that he wouldn't lie now. He clicked off his pencil light and stepped carefully back into the darkness keeping his gun pointed at the frightened pawnbroker. "Stay out of trouble Cash." As he faded away into the blackness of the alley he stowed away his gun and quickly made his way back to his car. Once there he powered away quietly, headed for home. Tomorrow would be a busy day.

The next morning Doc Murdock put robberies and jewels out of his mind to concentrate on his clients. He spent the morning at his Swank Street clinic examining clients and doing consultations. After he had seen a wealthy woman out of the reception area he turned to Dale, "How would you like to do some window shopping with me during lunch?"

Dale raised an eyebrow, "What kind of shopping?"

Doc smiled, "I thought we might look at some jewelry."

Dale smiled back, "What girl could turn down an offer like that, after all, 'All that glitters isn't just gold.'"

Minutes later they were in Doc's roadster and cruising downtown. He found a parking spot and they began strolling along 3rd Street. Doc stopped in front of a window that proclaimed "DeRuyter's Fine Jewelry" in large gold letters painted on its surface. He took Dale's hand and said, "Let's look in here honey. There may be something you like."

As they entered, Doc's immediately noticed two workmen installing new glass in two waist high display cases. His attention was then drawn to the well-dressed man advancing toward them. The medium built, middle aged man had his hand out and a smile on his face, "Good afternoon folks, my name is Jonathan. How may I help you today?"

Doc shook the out stretched hand and spoke, "I thought we might look for a gift for my fiancé today. Are you the owner?"

"Yes, indeed, Jonathan DeRuyter at your service. I can see you don't need an engagement ring my dear. That is a lovely piece. Was it custom designed?"

Dale blushed demurely, "Yes, Miles had it designed especially for me." While this exchange took place, Doc took a careful look at the Jeweler. He was wearing a gold wedding band and had a firm but smooth grip. Trying to get a good look at his eyes Doc inquired, "Are you doing some remodeling?"

DeRuyter frowned, "I'm afraid we had some trouble a few days ago and unfortunately, some repairs were called for. Some our best stock is somewhat depleted, but I'm sure we can show the lady some very nice items. If you'll step this way miss. . ."

Doc feigned surprise, "Say, you aren't one of those jewelry stores that got robbed are you?"

The jeweler looked slightly pained as he nodded, "I'm afraid so."

Without prompting Dale pitched in quickly, "Oh, that must have been terribly frightening, was anyone hurt?"

Turning to the slim, young girl DeRuyter frowned, "Actually, I did not see much of anything. I was upstairs on the phone when it happened. I had no idea anything was wrong until I heard the alarm. I rushed down here but by then the robbers had left. Fortunately my staff handled things very well, and thank God no one was injured, just some physical damage," he waved his hand toward the workmen. He then led Dale toward a display case as Doc thought to himself, ...and the expensive jewelry that was stolen.

Fifteen minutes later they were waiting for Dale's not inexpensive purchase to be wrapped up when a slightly built man wearing glasses and an expensive suit entered the jewelry store carrying a briefcase. He strode directly up to DeRuyter who immediately recognized him, "Oh, Mr. Samuels. Do you have more questions for me?"

The smaller man nodded and opened his briefcase, "Yes, Mr. DeRuyter, before we can settle your claim we have to go over a few more items. Can we speak in private?" DeRuyter waved a friendly goodbye to Doc and Dale as he led the newcomer into the rear of the store. As Doc and Dale exited the store he thought about the insurance settlement that DeRuyter was obviously expecting.

The two did not return to Swank Street; instead they drove to the Down Street clinic where Doc had several appointments that afternoon. He saw several patients and by the time he had seen the last one to the front door, he looked at his watch and realized it was too late to make a trip to the other robbed jewelry store that day. Instead, he saw Dale to her car. When she inquired what he had planned for the evening, he just smiled. Knowing that her beloved was probably going into danger she kissed him and urged him to be careful. Doc made the trip back to Swank Street quickly and was calling for Tommy as he entered his apartment. Tommy met him coming out of the kitchen with a dish towel in his hand, "What's up Boss?"

I've got a new mission for you. But first, have you heard anything today?"

"Nope. Not a word, and I was out on the street a lot. Nobody's talking."

"Okay. We're going to try a new slant. I want you to start asking around quietly about Danley and DeRuyter; the two jewelers who were robbed."

Tommy's bugged out a little, "You suspect the jewelers?"

"Not necessarily, but I ran into an insurance man today who got me thinking. Just ask around about those two and see if anyone's talking about them. Maybe one of them might have some money troubles."

The little man set down the dish towel and turned for his coat, "I'll go and ask around tonight."

When Tommy had gone Doc moved to his study and sat at his desk. He mulled his next move for a few minutes until a thought came to him. He reached for the telephone and his address book at the same time. Quickly locating a number. he dialed and his call was answered on the third ring, "Hello."

"Hello Paul? Miles Murdock here. How are you?"

"Fine Miles, just fine. How is that engagement set holding up?"

"It's great and Dale just loves it. In fact I'm thinking of a wedding present to match it."

"So you've set a date then."

"No, we're still a ways off from that but it's never too early to start planning. I was wondering if I could come by soon and look at what you're working on, say tomorrow. Something might strike my fancy."

"Sure. Tomorrow's good. You know me. I get up late and work late. But why not this evening? I'll be here working for another hour or so."

Doc looked at his watch. It was barely six o'clock, "I could come by. How about half an hour?"

"Great, see you then."

Doc hung up, grabbed his hat and headed down to his car. The drive across town did not take long. Paul Sanford had been a jewelry store owner who had gone bankrupt after the crash. He had come to Akelton a few years ago. He had worked hard and saved his money. When he had paid off his debts, he began designing custom jewelry out of his home. He was talented and soon his reputation spread. Now he was selling to many of the jewelry stores in town as well as to well off customers such as Doc Murdock. He worked out of a modest office in a downtown building. He worked by himself and kept unusual hours. Doc found a parking place in front of the five story building and took the elevator to the fourth floor. He knocked at the door which had "Sanford Custom Designs" painted on the frosted glass. Immediately a voice called from within, "Is that you Doc?"

"It's me."

The lock turned and the door opened. Sanford was a trimly built, gray haired man of probably fifty years. His grip was strong as he shook Doc's hand, "Sorry, about the door but I keep it locked after hours."

"That's all right. You've got a lot of valuables lying around." He waved his hand toward the designer's long work bench that had several pieces of gold jewelry in various states of construction lying on it.

"Sure do. Take a look at what I'm working on now." He proceeded to show Doc several interesting pieces. They talked design for a while before Doc worked the conversation around to where he wanted. "I thought of you recently when I was in DeRuyter's jewelry the other day. I saw one of your designs and thought I'd give you a call."

"Oh yeah, he's bought a lot of my stuff over the years. It's tough about him getting robbed, isn't it? I mean he's sure had a string of bad luck lately."

Doc was immediately interested but kept his voice calm, "Yes, he was robbed a couple of days ago. But that might mean more work for you won't it? After all, he'll want to replace his stolen inventory as soon as his insurance company pays off."

Sanford shrugged, "I kind of doubt it. He hasn't bought anything from me in a while. I'm sure he's got other uses for any insurance money."

Casually Doc inquired, "Oh; Money problems?"

Sanford shook his head sadly, "Of a sort, it's his wife. I'm afraid she's gravely ill. She's been hospitalized for a while and the bills must be piling up."

Somewhat caught off guard by this revelation, Doc nodded, "That's terrible. I'm sorry to hear it."

The two chatted awhile longer and parted with Doc promising to bring Dale by to look at some designs. On the way home Doc thought grimly about what kind of desperate acts a man might commit in an effort to save his dying wife. He would make some calls tomorrow to some of his medical contacts to confirm this situation. If it was true, then DeRuyter would bear closer scrutiny.

A single desk lamp illuminated an expensive desk. Other than the lamp and a telephone the only item on the desk was a wadded up black velvet cloth that lay on the blotter. The rest of the room was in darkness. A door opened and was quietly closed. A lock clicked and a man's figure moved to the desk. Two hands moved into the light and unfolded the black cloth. Revealed was a mass of glittering gold and sparkling jewels. A hand sorted carefully through the obviously expensive jewelry. Diamond pendants were mixed with brooches and earrings of rubies and emeralds.

The leader sighed quietly. A good haul, he thought to himself. Things had been going well. Two jobs complete and everything on schedule until that stupid cop had wandered by. His right hand moved to his left arm and rubbed it gently. The idiot hadn't even been a good shot. He'd only managed to hit him with a ricochet. "Damn," he cursed quietly. His thoughts moved rapidly. He couldn't let things fall behind schedule. Moving quickly was his only defense. The sooner this was all finished the better. He reached for the phone. . .

Doc was kept busy the next morning seeing patients at Down Street. He did find time to make a couple of calls to medical colleagues about DeRuyter's wife, though. Medical ethics did not allow him to learn details about her condition, but he learned enough to confirm Sanford's story. DeRuyter's wife was very ill and had been for some time. As the noon hour approached, he called Dan Griffin at his office and spoke briefly to the captain. Doc asked him to pick him up for lunch at one p.m. Griffin, suspecting that Doc had knowledge to impart, quickly agreed.

Just before one o'clock Doc was waiting outside the clinic as Captain Griffin pulled up in his squad car. Doc hopped in and they pulled smoothly into traffic. Keeping his eyes on the road, Griffin growled, "Tell me you're not just angling for a free lunch."

Doc smiled, "I'll buy the lunch as long as you take me by Danley's first."

Griffin risked a quick glance at Doc. He raised an eyebrow and asked, "Why there?"

"I want you to tell him you stopped by to see if he had remembered anything new about the robbery. Explain my presence by telling them we're on our way to lunch." Before Griffin could ask Doc continued, "I want to get a close look at Danley and hear his voice."

A nod, "Okay, it's obvious that you suspect Danley. Care to tell me why?"

Doc quickly gave Griffin more details about the gunman's hands and voice. When Griffin questioned him about possible motives Doc replied, "Insurance. I've found out that DeRuyter is badly in need of money because of his sick wife. I'm working on a money motive for Danley now."

Griffin agreed to play along. In a few minutes they reached the scene of the latest robbery. Griffin parked along the curb in a red zone knowing no traffic officer would dare to ticket his cruiser. As they walked to the jewelry store, they immediately noticed two workmen maneuvering a new plate glass window into the large hole in the store front. They waited patiently until the way was clear and entered the store. A tall, well-dressed woman was watching the workmen with a critical eye. She turned toward them and began, "I'm sorry we're closed for repairs. Oh, it's detective uh…, Griffin, isn't it?"

Griffin smiled graciously, "Yes it is. I'm sorry to bother you again, Mrs. Danley, but we were passing by on our way to lunch and I thought I'd stop and see if you or your husband had remembered anything else about the robbery."

Mrs. Danley smiled, "Of course; let me get Robert he's just in the back." She turned and walked around a counter to the back room, "Robert, the police are here again. They want to ask us some more questions." There was an answering voice from the back and within seconds a well-built middle aged man in a dark suit entered the showroom. He immediately smiled and came toward Griffin with his hand outstretched, "Captain Griffin, it's good to see you. Do you have good news for us? Have you caught those thugs yet?"

Griffin shook the jeweler's hand and tried not to look uncomfortable, "I'm afraid not. I just thought we'd stop by and see if you or your wife had remembered any more details about the robbery."

The jeweler frowned, "That's too bad. We could use some good news." He waved a hand, "We still aren't able to reopen yet, probably tomorrow though." He turned toward Doc, "Is this one of your men? We haven't met yet." He held out his right hand, "I'm Robert Danley." Doc shook the proffered hand. As he met the firm grip he quickly sized up Danley. He too wore a wedding ring although it was more elaborate than DeRuyter's had been. He was about the same height and build as the thieves' leader but as Doc looked into his eyes he saw no sign of recognition. Before Doc could reply Griffin spoke up, "No, this is my friend Miles Murdock. We were just on our way to lunch when I decided to stop by."

Mrs. Danley spoke, "I'm afraid I haven't thought of anything I haven't already told you."

"No other details? Nothing at all?"

"I'm afraid not."

Griffin then turned an inquisitive look Danley's way. The jeweler shook his head, "As you know captain, I was out making a deposit at the bank. I wish we could help you but we haven't remembered anything else."

Griffin thanked the two and they made their exit, Doc nodding to the two victims as he left. Once in the cruiser Griffin growled at Doc as he stepped on the starter, "Well, anything?"

Doc replied thoughtfully, "He has the same build as the wounded gunman but then so did DeRuyter. There certainly was no recognition in his eyes when I shook his hand. Either he's got nerves of iron or he's not our man."

Griffin grunted as he pulled into traffic. After a pleasant lunch he dropped Doc back at the Down Street clinic where Doc picked up his car and drove to Swank Street. After seeing several patients, he closed the clinic early and went upstairs with Dale. They found Tommy waiting for them. Once in his study, Doc asked, "Did you find out anything about DeRuyter or Danley?"

"Well, Doc. You were right. DeRuyter's wife has been really sick. She's been in the hospital a long time, and I guess the bills are piling up."

"What about Danley?"

Tommy shook his head, "I haven't heard anything about him yet. I'm still asking around, though. But I did hear something else that may be important." Doc, raised an eyebrow, "And?"

"Well, I was talking to this guy last night who works for a collection agency. He mentioned something about a jewelry store owner that was in some money trouble. I perked up right away thinking it might be one of the guys you was interested in but it turned out it was someone else."

"Who?"

"Some guy named Hinshaw. He has a place over on 5th. The guy I talked to said he was in some bad money trouble. He was behind on his bills and might have to close his shop."

Doc rubbed his jaw thoughtfully. He turned to his desk but Dale was already reaching into a drawer to pull out a telephone directory. She leafed through it quickly and then looked up, "There's a *Hinshaw Fine Jewelry* on

5th." Doc glanced at his watch and nodded, "Tommy can you see that Dale gets home safely? And then wait here by the phone?"

"Sure Doc."

Tommy helped Dale with her coat. Before they left, she urged him to be careful. Once alone Doc went to his safe. Removing his Purple Scar mask, he secreted it in its hidden pocket; he also stowed away his revolver on his hip. Leaving by the back door, he drove downtown to 5th Street. It was just after 5 o'clock and traffic was fairly heavy. He eventually found a parking spot nearly a block away from the jewelry store and walked back to it. He wanted to get a look at Hinshaw up close hoping he might recognize him something about him. As with the other two jewelers he was also hoping for a reaction when Hinshaw saw his face.

Entering the store, he saw a young man being shown some items by a sales girl to his right. Behind a counter ahead of him a well-dressed middle aged woman was on the phone. He browsed the wedding sets under the glass counter until she ended her call and came forward.

"Hello, can I help you pick out something for that someone special?"

Doc came up with his best smile, "That would be nice."

As she opened the case and brought out a tray of rings Doc queried, "Is Mr. Hinshaw here? I was told to ask for him by a friend."

"I'm afraid he's not in at the moment. However, I'm Betty Hinshaw his wife." She held out her hand. Doc shook it and smiled, "I'm Miles Murdock."

A look of momentary recognition passed across her face, "You wouldn't be Dr. Murdock the well-known plastic surgeon would you?"

Keeping the smile on his face neutral, Doc slipped a quick glance at her left hand as he answered, "Why yes I am."

"Then it's a pleasure to meet you. You did some wonderful work on a friend of mine last year, Mary Pleasance?"

Doc vaguely recognized the name and replied with some polite comments. When Mrs. Hinshaw again asked to show him some jewelry he acquiesced and spent several minutes looking at some nice settings. Soon he pointedly looked at his watch, "I'm afraid I don't have much more time today. Perhaps I'll come back tomorrow when Mr. Hinshaw is here."

"He'll be sorry he missed you, Dr. Murdock. Please stop in again."

Smiling a pleasant goodbye, Doc left the store and strolled casually down the street toward his car. He paused with his hand on the passenger door, thinking, *Too bad.* He had hoped to meet Hinshaw and perhaps get a reaction from him. It was interesting that his wife had known who he was, though. Could she really know him through a previous patient? He would have to check his records.

Suddenly, he jerked his head up as a loud alarm bell began to sound. He instinctively looked toward the sound. Down the block in front of the jewelry store he saw a hooded man dive into the open door of black sedan double parked in front of it. The door slammed, and with a squeal of tires the sedan accelerated down the street. Caught off guard, Doc stood transfixed for a second as the getaway car roared toward him. Cursing to himself, he jerked the car door open and dove behind the wheel. As he pressed the starter the black sedan roared past, horn screaming. Engine started, Doc swerved into traffic, earning himself a horn blast from an offended driver. He ignored it and concentrated on catching the fleeing gunmen. He slowed as a traffic light turned red, glanced each way, judged he could make it and ran the red light with his own horn blaring. He swerved around a taxi, a street car and several autos as he powered through the city streets.

Within two minutes he had closed the distance to less than fifty yards behind the sedan. The pursuit had left the downtown area and entered a more residential neighborhood. Traffic had lightened and Doc gripped the wheel tighter. There were fewer cars on the streets but more pedestrians about. Ahead the sedan rounded a corner on two wheels. Doc slowed into the turn and started to accelerate but instead jammed both feet down onto the brake pedal. Ahead the sedan screamed down the street barely missing a woman pushing a carriage across the street. His coupe skidded to a halt a safe distance from the woman. Doc gave her a friendly wave and in return received as chilly a glare as he had seen in quite a while. Once clear he accelerated in pursuit again.

The sedan had gained a considerable distance on the pursuing coupe. It took all Doc's skills to again catch up with it. The pursuit had continued across town and reached the industrial area not far from the river. As Doc closed within thirty yards of the sedan, he tugged out his pistol. Just a little closer and he would chance a shot at one of the rear tires. Then over the rushing wind and roaring engine sounds came the lonely moan of a steam whistle; a loud whistle. Jerking his head to the right Doc was shocked to see the engine and cars of a freight train bearing down on the speeding vehicles. Ahead the sedan accelerated as the driver attempted to beat the speeding freight. For just an instant Doc considered the same but just as quickly realized that he wouldn't make it. For the second time he squashed the brake pedal to the floor. The roadster nosed own and Doc

"…a hooded man dove into…a black sedan."

wrestled with the wheel as it fishtailed wildly. Ahead the sedan bounced high across the raised railroad crossing. Whistle blowing continuously the cow catcher on the front of the mighty engine barely clipped the right rear corner of the sedan's bumper as it steamed past. Doc's car came to a stop sideways in the road less than ten feet from the tracks.

Pounding on the steering wheel Doc silently cursed his luck. The gang was getting away and he was helpless. Fortunately, this train wasn't a particularly long one. A minute later and Doc was once more in pursuit. A half mile further along he was forced to brake to a stop once more. The road he was traveling ended at a stop sign. Ahead was a row of small warehouses. To the left and right stretched a highway that he recognized as River Road. To the right the road wound along the river down into the port area. To the left it headed out of town eventually becoming the highway that followed the river to Chesterton. In both directions Doc had a good view and he could see no sign of the fleeing car. A mental flip of a coin sent him to the left. Almost immediately he passed a street to his right lined with more small warehouses. He slowed to look down it but saw nothing. He repeated this at the next three streets but saw nothing. Powering down River Road, he traveled for several miles looking for any sign of the sedan but came up with nothing.

Finally admitting defeat,, he turned around and returned to the warehouse area. It was now after six and most businesses were closed. Cruising past the warehouses he looked carefully for any sign of the fleeing hoods. He quickly noted that not all of the mostly featureless building fronts were warehouses. Many of them were smaller units that contained small industrial business such as auto repair or building contractors such as plumbers or electricians. He was just about to break off the search when he splashed into a large pothole. The streets in this district were rough and ill maintained. Doc braked and got out of the roadster to check for damage. His attention was caught by the wet track his tire left after it passed through the water filled pothole. He looked thoughtfully around before getting back into the car. Once more he drove through the warehouse streets but this time he drove slowly, leaning out of the car to look at the rough streets. He was soon rewarded. Not far from the turn onto River Road he found a fast drying track leading from a large pothole. He followed it until it faded away on a short row of small garages. Getting out of his car he looked around the businesses. Everything was closed. He finally saw a sign on one of the walls that read:

For rental info call Budget Auto Repairs
Matt Lewis

A phone number followed. Noting the number Doc returned to his car and turned for home.

Arriving back at Swank Street, he changed clothes into a cheaper, dark suit and made himself something to eat. He was just finishing when Tommy returned. "Hey, Boss, did you find out anything?"

"Yes, I saw the gang pull off another job at Hinshaw Jeweler's. I lost them, but I've got a line on them now and I need some information."

"Sure Boss, what da ya need?"

I want you to find out anything you can on a garage owner named Matt Lewis. He's got a repair shop off River Road. Find out if he's on the up and up. And I need you to find out where a hood named Freddy Larkin can be found."

"Hey, I know Larkin. He's a small time thief, a soft shoe and jimmy man, strictly small time."

"Good. Find out where he hangs his hat. I need to find him tonight. I'll be out for a couple of hours. Call me here after that." Tommy nodded his assent and left.

Before Doc left the apartment again he added a ring of master keys and a pocket flash to his pockets. Once again in his roadster, he motored leisurely back across town and out to the Warehouse area along River Road. He parked some distance down the road and walked back, ducking out of sight whenever a car passed. When he reached the street, he had seen the wet tire track on he slowed. The street of warehouses was totally dark. Using his pencil flash he began examining each business near where the track had been. He flashed his light through every dusty window and pried large doors apart until he could shine his light through the crack. After several minutes of searching, his light was reflected off shiny metallic paint. Releasing the door he looked around. The doors were unmarked and apparently opened on a relatively small garage space. Reaching for his master keys, Doc went to work on the lock. Two minutes later it clicked open. Spreading the garage doors wide, Doc once more turned on his light. Revealed in its beam was a four door black sedan. It had out of state plates. Smiling to himself Doc quickly searched the car. Aside from a couple of spent forty-five caliber casings the only interesting things were some white paper sacks discarded in the back seat. Doc decided they were the kind that held take-out food from restaurants.

Quickly closing the doors Doc re-locked them and was on his way minutes later. Once back in his apartment he thought about his suspects. He was fairly certain that one of the jewelers was behind the robberies. Both Hinshaw and DeRuyter apparently had serious money problems. Neither DeRuyter or Danley had shown any recognition when Doc had met them, as they should have if one of them had been the leader that Doc had worked on. Interestingly, none of the three had been at their stores when the robberies had taken place. His thoughts were interrupted by the ringing of the phone. It was Tommy. He had addresses for both Freddy Larkin and Matt Lewis. His last bit of information was very interesting; "The word around is that Lewis deals in stolen cars and car parts Doc. So be careful when you talk to him." Doc reassured Tommy before hanging up. He then headed for his car.

Matt Lewis lived in an apartment above a garage where he did supposed legitimate work in a rough neighborhood of run down businesses. Doc parked a block away. Before leaving his car he carefully arranged the scarred purple mask on his face. Assuring himself of his gun, keys and pencil flash he locked the car and drifted silently through the shadows. The garage showed no visible lights. The Scar ghosted down a narrow alley alongside it. Once behind the shop, he looked up and could see a shaded light in an upstairs window. Nodding, he turned to the narrow back door of the garage. The lock clicked back with the third of the master keys he tried.

Wary of an unoiled door he eased it open very gently but it made no noise. Once inside with the door closed firmly behind him, the Purple Scar turned on his pencil flash and looked around. One wall was lined with a long work bench covered in tools and parts. A car sat in the middle of the floor with the hood wings up. A dozen tires were stacked in one corner. A set of stairs ran up an inside wall to a second floor closed door. Other than the double garage doors there were two small doors on the first floor. One led to a bathroom and one led to a small front office. Moving silently around the garage the Scar quickly ascertained that not much work went on here. A thin layer of dust covered most of the tools and benches, the same for the car. Undoubtedly Lewis made his money elsewhere.

Locating a fuse box on the wall the Purple Scar opened it and used his light. The beam revealed hand written labels pasted next to the glass fuses. Reaching in, he unscrewed the ones marked "garage" and "office." He then picked up a heavy wrench and moved on silent feet to the bathroom. He positioned himself in the doorway and turned off his pencil light. Hefting the wrench he threw it across the darkened garage. It landed somewhere with a metallic clatter. It must have hit something else because there was additional noise as several items fell to the concrete. Pulling the door nearly closed, the Scar drew his revolver and waited silently. A few seconds later there was a flare of light above him followed by the clicking of a switch several times and muttered curses. Then a shouted voice, "Who's there? Speak up! I've got a gun." The voice was answered by silence. Another curse was heard and then silence. A minute later a beam of light shone from somewhere above partially illuminated the garage. Foot-steps descending the wooden staircase came next. Peering through the cracked doorway the Purple Scar saw a man descend to the floor and wave a flash light around. The back splash of the light showed something metallic in his right hand. He appeared to be barefoot and wore only a t-shirt above his trousers.

Waiting until the man was approximately ten feet away with his back turned the Purple Scar kicked open the door and turned on his pencil flash. In his raspy voice he grated out, "Drop that gun! Don't move!" The man spun around. The Scar leapt forward and brought his revolver down hard on the man's wrist just behind his thumb. The gun in his hand clattered to the floor. Pivoting at the waist, the Scar brought his gloved left hand up in a wicked left cross to the man's jaw. Grunting in pain, he staggered back and sat down hard. Fixed in the beam of light, he was simultaneously trying to hold his bruised jaw and numbed wrist. He was middle aged and balding. His pants were held up by suspenders that also held back his bulging stomach. The Scar lowered his flashlight and angled it up a bit so his fierce features could be seen in the back splash of the light's beam. As he caught sight of his captor the man's breath caught in his throat. Immediately perspiration sprang out on his forehead and he licked his lips. He looked like he wanted to speak but said nothing. The Purple Scar grated at him, "You know who am?"

The man managed a nod.

The flashlight focused directly on his face, "You're Matt Lewis."

Another nod.

"All right, you're going to answer some questions for me. And don't bother lying because I know most of what's going on already," the Purple Scar rasped out. "You're renting a garage out on River Road. To three guys; they drive a black sedan. Who are they?"

At these words Lewis' face paled even more, "Uh…I don't know. I just rent them space."

"You're lying!" A gloved hand thumbed the hammer back on his revolver.

"No! Honest Scar, they didn't tell me any names. They just wanted the garage, uh… and a car."

"You sold them a car? What kind of car?"

Lewis wiped the sweat from his face with a shaking hand, "A Ford, brown, kinda beat up."

"What about the men? Where are they staying?"

"I don't know." He held up a shaking hand in front of him, "No, really. They just showed up a couple weeks ago. They wanted garage space and a car that wouldn't draw much attention."

The Purple Scar paused as he thought this over. He stepped closer to the frightened garage man and whispered in a rough voice, "Tell me about the men."

Lewis took a breath and attempted to calm himself, "Well, uh… the big blonde guy did all the talking. He sounded like he was from up North, talked funny yah know. The others didn't say anything but they all looked tough. I seen their kind before."

"What did the other two look like?"

Well, the shorter one was just an average Joe, kinda mousey brown hair. The thin guy with the black hair was something though. He was as tall as the blonde guy but real skinny and he had the look, ya know."

"What look?"

Lewis looked slightly at a loss for words, "Dead eyes, like a wolf. I seen shooters up in Chicago have that look. Like an empty grave, yah know. Of the three of 'em, he's the one I wouldn't wanna cross."

The Scar thought about this as he asked, "And you don't know where they're hiding out at?"

No, I told you, they never say much. Look I'm telling yah, that's all I know."

The Purple Scar actually believed him. It fit too well. These hoods sounded like professionals. They wouldn't tell Lewis anything he didn't need to know. "All right, down on your stomach."

"What?"

"You heard me. Now!" The reluctant garage man did as he was told. When he was flat on the floor with his hands over his head, the Purple Scar stepped forward and kicked the discarded gun across the room and under a workbench. As he backed toward the rear door he rasped out, "I'm leaving now but I'll be watching you. If you try to warn anyone, I'll know it and I'll be back for you." A pause, "You ought to have a doctor look at that hand." At the door he flicked off his pencil light, slammed the door behind him and disappeared down the alley. He waited at the corner for a few moments but there was no pursuit. He then crept silently back down the alley until he could see the back of the garage again. All was quiet. The only light was still in the upstairs window. A few minutes later, it went out. Satisfied that Lewis was not going anywhere, the Purple Scar walked quietly back to his car.

The Scar realized there was a danger that Lewis could call and warn the gunmen, but he did not believe Lewis knew any more than he had said. Those kinds of men wouldn't have been foolish enough to let someone like Lewis know where they were staying. Still, now he knew who he was looking for. Now he just had to figure out where they were. Perhaps, his next visit might help.

It wasn't a long trip to the cheap tenement building where Freddy Larkin supposedly lived. He parked near the address Tommy had given him and looked the place over. It appeared to be a run-down apartment house. It was nearly midnight and the streets were empty. Pulling his hat down and his collar up, he left the car and found the alley behind the tenement. Two minutes of careful movement found him directly behind the building. There was a locked back door, but more interesting to the Purple Scar was the fire escape stretching up the rear of the building. Using his pencil light, he located a garbage can. He carefully leaned the lid against a wall and ignoring the noxious smells coming from within, he turned it over and placed it under the fire escape. Climbing atop it, he could almost reach the lowest rung. Flexing his legs, he made an easy jump to the lowest rung and clambered up hand over hand to the second floor landing. The few rusty creaks it gave off probably couldn't have been heard ten feet away. Since Larkin's room was 306, he continued up another flight of the metal stairs. The stairs groaned but the noise was minimal.

Once at the third floor window the Purple Scar peered carefully through the dusty window. Inside, he saw a dimly lit hallway. No one was in sight. Using the blade of a pocket knife he pushed the latch out of the way and carefully lifted the lower sash. Ducking his head he climbed through the window. In this part of the hall only one overhead bulb was burning and light was minimal. On silent feet he followed the door numbers around corners to 306. Once there, the Scar decided there was too much light for his taste, so he unscrewed one of the overhead light bulbs leaving this stretch of hall in shadows. He listened at the door but heard nothing. His master keys made quick work of the cheap lock.

The apartment was dark. The Purple Scar left it that way using only his shielded pencil light to scan the room. To his left was a kitchen alcove and door leading to a bathroom. The rest of the apartment was one large room containing a sagging bed and a few pieces of furniture. Using a chair to unscrew the overhead light bulb, the Scar then moved the same chair into the kitchen and settled into it. He sat totally in the dark, his pen light in one hand and revolver in the other.

The Purple Scar waited patiently for nearly an hour before he heard the creak of loose floor boards in the hall. He stood up. There came the scratch of a key in the lock. The door swung open. It opened toward the kitchen and the Scar was concealed in its shadow. In the dim light from the hallway he saw a man shaped figure enter, turn, and reach for the light switch with his left hand as he swung the door shut with the other. Taking two quick steps forward, the Scar gave the door a good solid kick. It tore out of the figure's hand, clipped the side of his face, and slammed shut with a bang. There was a curse and something heavy crashed to the floor.

Stepping toward the sound the Scar flicked on his pen light. Caught in the beam was a short, thin, pasty faced man dressed in rough clothing sitting on the floor. He tried to shield his eyes from the light's glare, "What the. . ."

The Scar's rasp cut him off, "Don't move Freddy? Stay quiet and I won't have to shoot you." The little man visibly paled at this but nodded. "Good. Now I need information and you're going to help me."

"Who are you?"

"I think you've figured that out, Freddy."

Trying to see around the glare of the light, the crook licked his lips and nodded.

"All right. The word going around is that you've seen some strange hoods in town. Is that right?"

A nod.

"How many were there and where did you see them?"

Freddy's eyes shifted and he hesitated before finally admitting, "Well, I was out at the *Blue Moon Diner* a while back and three guys came in. I didn't know 'em but I know their type."

"Yeah," the Purple Scar grated. "What type is that?"

"Tough guys. Shooters."

"Uh, huh. How do you know that?'

"They was all carrying rods. I could see 'em even through those fancy suits they was wearing."

"I think you figured that out, Freddy."

"And you didn't recognize any of them?"

"Naw. They was from out of town. I could tell from the way they talked."

The Purple Scar paused for a moment. The *Blue Moon Diner* was out on River Road a few miles north of the garage where they kept their car. "When was all this Freddy?"

"Uh, a week ago. No, a little longer; maybe eight or nine days."

"Anything else? Did you see which way they left or what car they were in?"

A shake of the head, "Naw. I left pretty soon after they got there."

The Purple Scar went silent. Freddy misinterpreted this and began to whine, "Look that's all I know, really." As he backed toward the door and grabbed the knob with one hand, the Purple Scar's dropped his voice to a rough whisper, "That's all Freddy. But I'll be back if you've lied to me. Don't follow me and don't say anything about me being here." He stepped through the door and pulled it closed after him. As he moved quietly toward the rear fire escape he smiled to himself. He knew full well that Freddy would spread the word about his visit from the Purple Scar all over town and the underworld's fear of him would only grow.

Once out of the building, he made his way to his roaster and powered quickly away. Removing his mask, he headed back to Swank Street already planning how to use the clues he had collected. Tomorrow would be another busy day.

The leader sat behind his desk. In one hand he held a glass of whiskey. With the other hand he poked absently at a pile of gold chains, and expensive jewelry. As he sipped, he thought, *Well, that was the last one.* The robberies were over and the take had been good. It hadn't been totally smooth, though. In addition to his being winged, now that doctor was sniffing around. Undoubtedly the police were suspicious and had sent him around to see if he recognized anyone. He paused with the glass half way to his mouth, unless. . . someone had followed them today. Not the police. But who? Setting his glass down the leader rubbed his chin. If someone else had taken a hand and was using this doctor, it was just as well that the robberies were done. He would make the final split with the Chicago boys tomorrow night. Once they were gone, he could take his time changing his share into cash. His debts were getting serious, but the insurance money should come fairly quickly. Yes, it was going to be all right. Tomorrow would see an end to it.

+++

Doc Miles spent the next morning at the Down Street clinic seeing patients. He had Dale cancel all his afternoon appointments. Once finished there, he headed home and spent some time in his studio making up a new mask and putting together the gear he would need. He changed into an inexpensive and somewhat worn suit and stopped by his office long enough to take his Purple Scar mask from the safe. He was just leaving when the phone rang. It was Tommy, "Hey, Boss, I been trying to get you for a while."

"Sorry, Tommy. I've got a line on the hoods and I'm on my way now to find them."

"But I got news."

"Oh. . . what did you find out?"

"Well, I been asking around and there's lots of talk today."

"What kind of talk?"

"Well, I guess it's gotten around that the Purple Scar has taken a hand in these hold-ups. The word is he's rousting people and he wants these mugs bad. I guess a lot of shady characters are looking for holes to climb into. Anyway, I heard a couple of mugs joking about how Joe Kelly was taking odds on how it would go when the Purple Scar caught up to the new hoods in town and I got to thinking it might be good idea to check out what Kelly might know." Doc nodded as he listened. It was well known that Kelly ran the biggest book in town. He took bets on most sporting events especially horse racing. It was also reported that he had contacts with private gambling houses.

Tommy continued, "So I dropped around Kelly's betting parlor and asked a few questions. It turns out that one of those jewelry guys was a gambler." Doc perked up at this, "Which one?"

"Danley. It turns out that he likes the ponies. Slow ones though. I guess he's in deep hock to Kelly, and the word is he owes other bookies as well. I thought you'd like to know.

Doc assured him the information was important and was about to hang up when he asked, "Tommy, what about those odds? Was Kelly actually making book on the Purple Scar?"

Tommy chuckled, "You mention the Scar's name in a place like Kelly's and people start looking for rocks to crawl under. You be careful out there Doc."

Doc assured him he would and made for his car. He drove to River Road and followed it to the *Blue Moon Diner* just past the edge of town. It was just after noon and there was a good lunch crowd there. He saw no brown Fords. Turning around, he parked at the edge of the gravel parking area and went in. He was wearing the new mask he had just completed. It was of a bland, pleasant faced man. With his hair slicked back from his forehead and a thin mustache glued to his lip, no one would recognize him, he hoped, or be suspicious. He took a seat at the counter and ordered coffee and lunch. Looking around the diner, he mainly saw working men or travelers. He seemed to blend right in. There was no sign of the three men he sought. The lunch traffic thinned out as he lingered over coffee. Eventually, he paid and left.

The Scar drove perhaps a quarter mile down the road and pulled to the side of the road. He positioned his car so he could watch the distant diner and settled in to wait. He had brought binoculars and could easily get a good look at any car that pulled into the diner's parking lot. Time passed. The diner settled into the afternoon lull and there wasn't a lot of traffic in or out, but every car was given a good scrutiny through the binoculars. At five o'clock he drove back to the diner. He used the restroom and had coffee at the counter. While there, he casually inquired about dinner and how busy they might be. The counterman replied they usually had a good crowd for dinner. The Scar soon left and resumed his watch from down the road. Sure enough traffic soon picked up at the diner. By six p.m. they were quite busy. The Scar scrutinized every car but didn't see the one he wanted. By seven it was dark and dinner traffic had thinned out a bit. The diner parking lot was not very well lit and he was considering moving closer when a car entered the parking lot. Through the binoculars the Scar decided it looked a lot like a brown Ford. A single man left it and entered the diner. Starting the roadster he drove down the road and pulled over less than a hundred yards away from the diner. Through the binoculars the Ford certainly appeared to brown in color even in the dim light. Waiting patiently, the Scar was rewarded fifteen minutes later by the view of a man in a well-fitting suit returning to the Ford with an arm load of white sacks. Starting the roadster, he was ready as the Ford pulled out on the road and headed away from town.

Pulling out after it, the Scar drove carefully without lights, tracking his prey by the car's tail lights. Within minutes he saw the brake lights flash and the tail lights turn off the road. He slowed where he figured the car had turned off. Sure enough there was a battered mailbox at the edge of a gravel driveway leading through the trees. Noting the address, he turned into the drive and proceeded slowly up the gravel road. Quickly the trees thinned and the Scar could see the lights of a large house ahead. It sat in the middle of a large clearing scattered with trees and shrubs. Light spilled from several windows on both floors. Leaving the gravel, Doc drove quietly across some of the overgrown lawn and under a large tree. In the deep shadow under low tree limbs he killed the engine and listened. Normal night noises came to his ears; crickets chirping, an owl hooting and the distant sound of music from the house.

Quickly stripping off his mask, he then replaced it with the shocking countenance of the Purple Scar. His suit pockets contained his pencil flash and master keys. He checked his revolver in its hip holster and for good measure dropped some extra cartridges into his pocket as well. All indications were the men he was about to brace were experienced gunmen. He hoped to take them alive but was prepared to do what he had to if they resisted. Leaving the car, the Scar made his way carefully across the overgrown grounds. Away from the car, he looked back but could see nothing of it in the deep shadow and tall grass under the tree. He made little sound as he neared the house.

Once near the house, the Purple Scar realized the music he was hearing must come from a radio. It was dance music of some kind broken by commercials. He drew his gun and carefully circled the house. There were downstairs lights on in several rooms, but they had curtains drawn. The kitchen was bright with light and he could see that it was empty. He was about to continue around the house when a man entered the kitchen from an interior room. The Scar knelt down in the grass. The man crossed the kitchen and rummaged in a refrigerator. He was a tall, blond man in shirt sleeves rolled up to the elbows, his tie loose. A large automatic nestled in a shoulder holster beneath his left arm. He eventually came up with two brown bottles, opened them with a bottle opener and exited the room with one in each hand. Grimly nodding to himself that he had come to the right place the Scar continued around the house. He could see into no other windows on the ground floor. There were lights in two of the upstairs rooms; possibly bedrooms. Back at the front of the house he decided to try the front door. Going in the back door meant entering through a brightly lit room into who knows what. At least the front part of the house appeared dark.

Once on the shadowy front porch, he moved to the door and tried the knob. It turned beneath his grip. Carefully he turned the knob and pushed the door open a few inches. Dim light appeared around the jamb. Opening it a little more, he looked in. Ahead was a dimly lit hall leading to the back of the house. Wide stairs ran up the left side of the hall to the second floor. To his right was a darkened parlor partially illuminated from an unseen lighted doorway. To his left were closed sliding doors. He slid the doors open silently and found himself in a large darkened room lit only from light coming through the curtained windows. The Scar chanced his light for a brief moment. Furniture including a piano covered by white sheets and glass bookcases met his eye. He could hear the music more clearly now and see a thin band of dim light coming from under a closed door. Moving to the door he took off his hat and pressed his ear against it. Music and muffled voices came through the panel but not in the next room from the sound of it. Replacing his hat, he carefully turned the knob and pulled the door open. He could clearly hear the music now and the sounds of men talking amongst themselves. Listening for a few moments, he decided the men were playing cards. He could hear money clinking and the slap of cards on a hard surface.

Easing into the room, the Purple Scar found himself in a library. It was dark, the only illumination coming from a half open door ahead from which the voices were coming. To his right a closed door probably opened to the hall. He moved forward and pressed himself next to the partially open door. It opened inward but away from him. Half open he could easily shove it aside and be in the room before they knew it. With luck he could take them all alive. Taking a breath the Scar brushed the door wide open with his left hand and stepped in to the room with his gun up and pointed.

The room was the dining area. To his right there was an open door leading to the darkened hall. Ahead was an open door to what appeared to be a shelved pantry. To his left, under the window stood a waist high cabinet covered with empty white sacks and plates of food. The center of the room was dominated by a circular table with four chairs surrounding it. The chair to the right was occupied by the tall blond man; he was holding cards in his left hand. His right hand held a beer bottle halfway to his lips. Directly across the table from the Scar sat a short forgettable man also holding cards. He too was wearing an automatic in a shoulder holster. The tall thin man stood next to the cabinet, a plate in his left hand. A holstered gun was on his right hip within easy reach.

All this the Purple Scar saw in a brief second as he rasped out, "Nobody move!" That was the only order he got to give. Everyone went for their guns at the same instant. They were fast. Remembering the words of the frightened garage owner, the Purple Scar fired first at the thin man on his left. His gun had cleared the holster and was already coming level when the Scar's bullet hit him in the chest. His return shot tore through the Scar's jacket just over his hip barely missing him. The hood across the table shoved backwards, knocking his chair over as he jerked his automatic clear of its holster. His heel caught on the chair and his first shot went into the table exploding a bottle of beer. His second went up into the ceiling as he fell backwards. The Purple Scar threw two quick shots at the falling man. The first shot might have clipped his arm. His second shot went into the opposite wall. Pivoting and ducking side-ways the Scar exchanged shots with the large gunman on his right. Their first bullets crossed paths. The Scar felt a sting in his left arm. His shot missed and he fired twice more, both bullets crashing into the big gunman's chest. The mortally wounded hood fell backward, his pistol discharging upward into the crystal chandelier.

Purple Scar jerked back into the library doorway to reload. As he ejected the spent shells from his gun, he glimpsed the remaining gunman ducking into the open pantry across the room. Purple Scar slid into a crouch as he thumbed fresh cartridges into his gun. As he did, three bullets crashed through the wall above him. Reloaded, he leaned around the doorframe and fired into the wall of the pantry. An arm reached around the pantry door and returned fire; once, twice and then silence. There was a long pause and then the Scar watched as an arm reached out from the darkness of the pantry. An automatic dangled from a finger through the trigger guard; the slide locked back. A voice called out, "Don't shoot. I give up." A pause then, "I'm hit, I'm bleeding."

The Purple Scar rasped out, "Throw the gun out and come out with your hands up."

The automatic was tossed out and landed with a clatter. The gunman came forward out of the pantry with his hands in the air. His left shirt sleeve was red with blood. He was tight lipped and in obvious pain. The Purple Scar stepped forward into the light. When he saw the horrific features of his opponent the gunman paled even more but said nothing. Flicking his gaze left and right to the unmoving hoods the Scar then rasped out, "Where's your boss?" The wounded hood shook his head, "Not here. He's supposed to come later to make the final split."

Interested, the Scar repeated, "Final split?'

The gunman nodded, "Yeah, he called and said we're done. We were gonna head home tomorrow."

The Purple Scar stepped forward and asked in a harsh whisper, "Who is he?"

Before the wounded man could answer a shot barked out. The gunman jerked and started to collapse. Out of the corner of his eye, the Scar saw a flash of light from the darkened hall. He fired into the darkness as he leapt forward into the cover of the dining table. Underneath he could see the fallen gunman clutching his chest obviously hit hard. Lunging forward, the Scar reached the hall in four long strides. He got to the darkened hall in time to see a figure silhouetted in the open front doorway. He tried a snap shot but knew he missed even as the figure ducked through. Running out onto the front porch, he saw a dark figure running for the trees. He brought up his revolver in a two handed grip and took aim but hesitated. It was dark and the distance too great for that kind of shot. Instead he leapt down the steps and started running. He was only half way across the lawn when he heard a car start. Through the trees headlights came on and an engine revved as a car tore away in the darkness.

The Scar looked to his right to where his roadster was hidden and then back toward the house. Shaking his head he jogged quickly back to the house. Once in the dining room, he holstered his gun to check the wounded gunman. His eyes were closed and he was breathing shallowly. The Purple Scar ripped open his shirt to examine the wound. It was bleeding but not heavily. The real problem, he judged, was shock. Standing up, he grabbed a cloth napkin from the table and pressed it to the wound. Unbuckling the unconscious man's belt, he looped it tight around his chest and pulled the rough bandage tight against the wound. He then wrapped another napkin around the gunman's bleeding arm. A suit jacket knocked to the floor was placed under the hood's head. Then pulling another jacket off the back of a chair, he wadded it up and placed it under the man's feet, elevating them off the floor. The Scar stood up and searched through the drawers of the large cabinet under the window. He found china, flatware and eventually a table cloth. He quickly wrapped it around the man to keep him warm.

Satisfied that he had done what he could, the Scar searched for a telephone. Turning on lights, he found one on a stand in the hall. Using a more normal voice, he quickly connected with the operator. Giving her the address of the isolated house, he requested police and an ambulance. When she questioned his identity, he quickly hung up. Back in the dining room he checked the wounded man's pulse. It was weak but regular. Not good but at least he was alive. The Scar waited with the man for nearly five more minutes. Finally, looking at his watch he decided it was time to go. He hurried out of the house and across the lawn to his concealed car. Firing up the powerful engine he quickly made his way down the main road. Flicking on his headlights he turned toward town. Less than a minute later a police car passed him going the other way. A minute later it was followed by an ambulance. The Purple Scar pressed down on the accelerator. He had business in town that would not wait.

His destination was in one of the nicer residential sections of town. The Purple Scar parked his roadster on the street in the shadows of a huge maple tree. Slipping out of the car he worked his way along the sidewalk to a large two story house in mid-block. The only lights on were downstairs on one side. Easing his way to that side of the house and taking cover behind a tree, he could see into the room. It appeared to be some kind of office or study. As he watched, a middle aged man in a suit entered, walked to the window and immediately pulled down the window shade shutting off the view of the room. No matter. The Scar had recognized his man.

Moving to the front porch, he found the front door locked. He reached for his keys. The fourth key he tried turned in the lock. Easing the door open he slipped inside, his reloaded revolver in hand. The entire lower floor was in darkness. The only light came from a thin band of light under a door further down the front hall. Gliding through the darkness the Purple Scar arrived at the door and listened carefully. He could hear a low one-sided conversation. That ended with a "Good bye" and the click of a telephone being put down.

Not taking a chance on the door being locked the Purple Scar raised his left leg and gave the door a powerful kick just above the knob. It crashed open and the Scar stepped into the doorway. The room was a study. Books lined the two walls. Comfortable armchairs faced a large desk. The only light came from a shaded lamp on the desk. Other than a telephone the only other thing on the desk was a scattering of glittering jewelry. The man seen through the window was leaning over the desk. He straightened and stared at the fearsome figure before him. He didn't blanch in fear but his mouth drew together in a thin line of stress. His revolver steady, the Scar rasped out, "Don't move Danley!"

The jeweler didn't move. In a quiet voice he acknowledged, "The Purple Scar."

"That's right. It's all over now. Your gunmen are all dead and the police will be here for you soon. I'd ask you why you did it—but I know why. So just put up your hands." Danley slowly raised his hands. "Now step out here and sit down." As Danley stepped around the desk with his hands raised, he deliberately brushed the lampshade with his left elbow. The lamp spun off the desk, turned over and landed on the floor next to the desk. The bulb did not break but with the only light in the room now on the floor the study was thrown into deep shadow. As this was happening, Danley threw himself to the right, his hand darting for a pocket. The Purple Scar yelled, "Don't. . ." and fired. Danley staggered but still managed to jerk a revolver from his pocket. The Purple Scar's next shot struck him squarely in the chest. Danley's gun fired; the bullet slamming into the floor. The jeweler's gun dropped to the floor as he fell forward onto the desk. Hands outstretched, he grasped at it for support as he slid to the floor but all he managed to grasp was a handful of jewelry. He hit the floor with a groan and rolled over onto his back the glittering jewelry spilling across his blood stained chest.

Kneeling over the dying man, the Purple Scar leaned down and whispered, "You didn't have a chance."

Danley attempted a weak smile and whispered, "Had to try," and died.

The Scar stood up and listened for a moment, but all was quiet. Holstering his gun, he moved to the phone. A quick call connected him to police headquarters. He called for officers and urged the notification of Captain Griffin. Setting down the receiver, he left the house with the front door wide open. He was in his roadster and blocks away before the first squad car, siren screaming arrived at Danley's home.

The next day was a busy one for Doc Miles at both the Down Street clinic and then at his Swank street office. The bullet wound on his left arm was just a scrape and would heal quickly, so he kept to his appointment schedule. Day finished, he had finally settled behind his desk and leaned back for a moment before Dale bustled in. She held a newspaper.

"Have you seen the headlines?' Doc shook his head. Dale's eyes sparkled mischievously as she read, "Jewelry gang smashed. Police state that three suspects are dead and one is in custody after a round up of the violent gang. Further, a local business man was apparently connected to the recent robberies." She paused and looked up at Doc, "Good press. . .for the police."

He waved a hand. "They deserve it. I had a talk with Dan Griffin late last night. We decided this would be the story. Best to keep the Purple Scar's name out of it."

Dale nodded, "Was he surprised that Danley was behind it all?"

"He was. I wasn't."

Just how did you know it was him?"

"Well, I figured early on it was probably an insurance scam. I suspected Danley but wasn't sure until Tommy came through with a motive for him. It turns out he was quite a gambler. He owed several bookies and even a loan shark. They were pressuring him. He brought in some hired guns in to rob himself and collect the insurance. That would pay off his debts. His cut of the stolen loot could be kept and sold off piecemeal when suspicion had died down."

"And the other robberies?"

"Just a smokescreen to spread suspicion around. Danley knew they had money troubles too. Of course the extra loot was nice for him."

"But you suspected him before Tommy heard about the gambling. Why?"

Doc smiled, "The leader took off his wedding ring during the robberies. DeRuyter and Hinshaw wore plain gold bands, very common. Danley's was a more elaborate custom design. I saw it on his finger. It was easily identifiable. By the way, Dan Griffin says they've arrested his wife too. Apparently she was in on the plan."

Dale frowned, "So in the end, Danley was given away by his own jewelry."

With a small smile, Doc just nodded.

THE END

THE RETURN OF THE PURPLE SCAR

've said before that I've always considered the masked avenger pulps to be my favorites. I always saw the mysterious heroes and their alter egos as the epitome of the pulps. What did I like about them? Was it the secret identities? The masks and costumes? The fact that they always operated outside of all authority? I don't know, but I do know that it was always the Shadow dealing out justice with his twin .45s while laughing mirthlessly that I daydreamed about. Or maybe it would be The Black Beauty speeding through the night carrying the Green Hornet and Kato on a new mission or the Spider saving the nation from some fiendish deadly plot.

At any rate, to me, the masked avengers were always the royalty of pulp heroes and when I began writing new pulp, those names were at the top of my list to write about, if I got the chance. Now a lot of the best known heroes are copyrighted and permission is needed to publish work about them, so when I was given the chance to write about a lesser known avenger like the Purple Scar, I jumped all over it. After all, any masked avenger is still an exciting character, even one I had never heard of before. I read all the original Purple Scar adventures, thought about him a bit then sat down and cranked out *Liquid Death* for Airship 27's first volume of the Purple Scar. It wrote quickly and turned out to be a good little story that I'm quite proud of. Soon enough, though, I moved on to other writing projects and didn't think much about it. So a while back I was looking through my writings for some references and came across *Liquid Death*. I sat down and read it fresh for the first time in eight months and realized not only what a good story it was but just how much fun I'd had writing it.

So in a fit of nostalgia I started imagining other Purple Scar adventures. I liked the dichotomy of the Scar's life; gentle healer during the day and dark avenger at night. So I got to thinking; what would happen if one of his lives spilled violently over into the other? This happened just as I was watching a detective show about a certain scam, and *voila* a plot materialized. Before I knew it, I was at my keyboard writing another Purple Scar adventure. I found it was like writing about an old friend. I knew just what the Scar (or Miles Murdock) would do and just how to fit other characters in around him. Not to mention how familiar the city of Akelton had become to me. I found I had pictured how the city was laid out and where the important landmarks were. So almost before I knew it, *All that Glitters is Death* had rolled off my keyboard.

The question was what to do with it. It felt right and I enjoyed writing it, but I had written it just for my own entertainment without thought of publication, I was unsure if Ron at Airship 27 would be interested in it at that moment. I knew he was still knee-deep in getting out the first volume of the Purple Scar (not to mention all of the other ongoing projects at Airship 27) so I was unsure if he wanted a story for a second volume. Fortunately he was interested. No doubt he has the same faith and interest in the Purple Scar as I do. That's a good thing as there are lots of great possibilities for this wonderful character.

So here it is. More adventures of everyone's favorite (I hope) masked avenger. I hope you like it. It sure was a lot of fun to write. I'd stay tuned though; I have a feeling we're going to see a lot more of our intrepid avenger in the future.

It was great to revisit the Purple Scar as a writer. I know he is certainly not my personal property because other fine writers are now chronicling him with their own takes on his interesting adventures. But I like him and I will say this: I am not jealous of the writers re-imagining the adventures of the Green Hornet or the Shadow. After all, who needs to write about the Spider when you can write about the strange adventures of the Purple Scar? So in the end I may have found my own masked avenger. Maybe now I'll be day dreaming about the Scar sneaking down alleys to terrorize the underworld. . . I could do a lot worse.

GENE MOYERS - studied European and Medieval history at the University of Oregon. He is a former U.S. Army armor crewman. He worked in the High Tech industry for some time and ran a store front and internet hobby shop for several years.

An avid military gamer and role player, his favorite game was *Daredevils* set in the 1930s. His love affair with the 1930s and pulps in particular stem from his first time reading a *Shadow* novel as a boy. Although interested in writing since a teen, he did not turn to serious writing until 2000. He is the co-author of *GURPS Crusades* published by Steve Jackson Games. He has written a story for *Ravenwood* volume II as well as a story for the second volume of *Moon Man* and a *Purple Scar* adventure all for Airship27. When not working on Airship 27 projects he is busy writing horror adventures for his swashbuckling character set in Colonial America.

Gene currently lives in Beaverton Oregon with his wife and three lazy dogs.

PRESCRIPTION FOR THE MOB

BY PAUL KEVIN FINDLEY

"**T**hat was good work on the construction worker's arm, Bill. The scar from the sutures should be minimal."

"Thank you, Dr. Murdock. I appreciate your help, but it galls me to have another physician hovering over my shoulder just to watch me stitch a simple cut. Even worse, I need you to write prescriptions for my patients in my own clinic."

"I understand, but until we can get you approved by the state licensing commission, this is the best we can do. I'll be back on Friday; if you do have any emergency work past simple exams or handing out pamphlets, be sure to mark it down in your book for that day. Call me if that happens so we can keep our stories straight."

The tall physician motioned toward the back, "I'm going to clean up and get ready to leave. I have a rather important date that will not appreciate being stood up again."

William Everett simply smiled and nodded in sympathy.

As he finished, Miles Murdock heard an argument taking place. Not wanting to interfere if it was a patient, the respected plastic surgeon cracked the washroom door just enough to hear, ready to close it if the subject was personal medical details.

"I'm telling you, Doc, you need protection in this neighborhood."

"These are my people, Maxie; I take care of them and they take care of me. The only people who'll smash my windows are going to look like you."

"Aww don't be like that, Doc. Mr. Parker takes good care of everybody who pays him; just like he takes care of those who don't." He spread his arms out, "I'll make sure you wouldn't even have to pay! Just look out for any special clients the Boss might send your direction."

The voice was familiar, so Miles Murdock opened the door just enough to look down the short hallway and into the waiting area. The goon was no one the doctor would ever admit to knowing, but he certainly did. Maxie

Smith had escaped justice on several occasions; he was even one of the few to escape from the Purple Scar's bullets last month.

Everett frowned. "Gunshot and stab wounds no one wants to explain?"

"Now you're getting the idea Doc! If you agree to help us out every now and then, Mr. Parker can make sure the city's recommendation board gives you a thumbs-up to the license commission just like that." Maxie snapped his fingers on the last word.

"That's fine for you and Dell Parker. It only works for me until some do-gooder on the city council shuts me down because of 'irregularities' in my license. Are you two going to appear on my behalf at City Hall or State Court?"

"That's what lawyers are for, Doc! Mr. Parker is more of a behind the scenes guy, a philanthropist! He'll make sure you've got a mouthpiece worth his salt, though."

The young doctor shook his head. "Sorry, Maxie, there's not enough for me to even think about getting in bed with your boss."

Maxie's smile went brittle and his voice down half an octave. "You need to think again, Doc. Mr. Parker has big plans for the Westside." He stabbed his finger in Everett's chest and then turned to leave. "Make sure you're part of them."

Once the door closed behind Smith, Doctor Murdock stepped out of the washroom and moved quickly to a window. He saw the thug drive off in a powerful sedan and then turned to confront Everett.

"Bill, was that Maxie Smith? I saw his picture in the papers after that incident on the docks last month. The police are still looking for him."

"Doctor Murdock, you can't report this to them. Any investigation is going to kill my application with the city recommendation board and bring down this clinic. Where are my people going to get medical care then?"

"There are clinics all over Akelton City."

"Yes, nearly all of them staffed by white doctors who have to make a negro grandmother in the middle of an asthma attack wait behind a white lady there to get an ointment for dry skin. If he doesn't and someone complains, then he stands to lose his license!"

"Those are rare occurrences Bill and you know it."

"Not to her family it wasn't! I went to the funeral last week!" Everett threw up his hands and began looking around the exam room. "Fine then, at least give me two days to clean out the office and disappear. I can show up again in a few weeks somewhere else; maybe Mulberry Street."

"Bill, if you disappear now, the board will never recommend you to practice in Akelton City or anywhere else; you'll lose everything you've worked for. Let's both take a step back and think about this for a moment. It's almost seven o'clock; is there another business nearby that Smith might have gone to in order to threaten?"

William snapped his fingers. "The Hot Spot Club is just a few streets over. His boss, Dell Parker, owns the liquor license for it, which means he owns the club. Maxie probably went in there for a couple of free drinks and to stash his take before the dance halls start jumping around nine. He looked like he was dressed for a night out, not strong-arming merchants."

"Stash his take?"

The younger physician nodded. "Parker uses the club as a temporary 'bank' before spreading the money all over town." William held up a hand. "Before you say anything else, this is the Westside; lots of open secrets around here that people just ignore to get along."

'A very useful bit of information' was all Miles Murdock thought however. Rousing himself, he responded to William Everett. "All right then, I can tell the police I saw him there and not mention the clinic at all." Dr. Murdock hesitated before he asked, "Is this a place where I can go in and not stick out?"

Everett grinned at his fellow physician's discomfort. "Are you trying to ask me if white folk that aren't criminals can just walk right in?"

Embarrassed, the senior doctor replied, "Well, yes. It would be best if I actually saw Maxie in the club, but I don't want to attract attention or otherwise cause a problem."

"Ha ha ha! You'll be okay, Doctor Murdock. The Hot Spot has some of the best music in town. Now, what will you do when you get in the club?"

"I'll stay there just long enough for one drink and leave. I've mentioned before about my friend Captain Griffin. I can talk to him and leave out any mention of the clinic; just tell him that I saw Maxie sitting at the bar and leave it at that."

"Then you should simply call Captain Griffin now. Maxie Smith is not a man to pursue Doctor Murdock."

"I have to make sure he's there, otherwise Griffin will order out a lot of officers for nothing. Are you certain Maxie will go there?"

The younger doctor looked thoughtful for a moment. "Most likely yes; Maxie likes the Hot Spot and not just for the free drinks. He likes to pretend he's a patron of the arts or something." Smiling now, "You're not exactly dressed for a dance hall Doctor; better catch him there."

"I'll go now; wish me luck."

"Good luck."

Outside the clinic and unseen by William Everett, Miles Murdock placed his medical bag in the trunk of his automobile and then opened an identical one. From it, he withdrew a sap and a long barreled .38 which he placed in his coat pockets. He also carefully took out a small leather case. This contained the talented doctor's other identity, one not bound by the Hippocratic Oath. The only oath this man recognized was vengeance; the vengeance of the Purple Scar.

He removed the visage of his late brother's death face and tucked it away in a hidden pocket in his suit coat. Then he quickly removed a second mask and placed it over his face. This mask the doctor made as nondescript as possible. Once it was firmly in place, he closed the trunk and then drove to the Hot Spot.

Maxie was finding it difficult to relax that night. Despite a heavy take from local businesses, it was Everett's refusal to play ball with Mr. Parker that had his attention. Usually, the gang boss would have had someone start leaning on a family member to force a mark in line. Everett, though, had no surviving family and was too busy with his new practice to see anyone.

The young doctor couldn't be bribed either. His parents had done well and left everything to their only child. That left burning out the clinic, but Mr. Parker had told Maxie no fires. He needed doctors in place the Westsiders already trusted.

BAM! The thug slammed his glass on the bar, then looked at the bartender, daring him to say anything. Sammy knew better; he just handed Maxie a new glass to replace the now broken one on the bar.

"Why can't Everett see how much Mr. Parker can do for him? Getting him past the board would only be the beginning." In frustration, the gangster raised his glass, ready to smash it on the bar just like its predecessor.

"That's a neat trick, friend."

"Huh?" Maxie looked at the man seated next to him and began to forget his face immediately. "What do you mean?"

"Break a glass and then hypnotize the bartender into giving you another one instead of calling the cops. Ha! I'd pay you to learn that one!"

"Buzz off, pal. I'm in no mood to play professor."

"Aw I didn't mean nothin', buddy. Let me buy you a drink, OK?"

"I ain't got time for this." Maxie muttered to himself and then got up to leave. He arrived at the coat check before the counter girl could get there. The angry goon reached over the gate and grabbed for his coat, knocking the rack to the floor.

"Hey you schmuck I'm on the hook for ...!" The girl's words stopped as Maxie grabbed her by the throat with his free hand.

"You wanna go home tonight, little girl, then shut it!" As he pushed his face into the scared woman's and continued to threaten her, the Purple Scar slid around behind him and went out the front door unnoticed. It closed moments before Maxie let her go and turned to leave.

The disguised vigilante had just ducked down behind Maxie's sedan when the thug walked out of the club. He slid the sap from his coat pocket and started moving as Maxie began to climb through the driver's door.

"I'll have Danny fire that broad tomorrow" he muttered to himself, "then I'll pay her a visit and see how much she wants her job back." He barely heard the footsteps behind him and turned his head in time to see the face from the bar before the sap put out his lights.

Waking slowly, Maxie remembered getting hit over the head. He couldn't understand though why his legs hurt, but his feet were numb. After another moment, he realized he was hanging upside down.

"Hey! Whoever you are, I'm Maxie Smith and I work for Dell Parker! Let me go now and you'll only get your legs broken."

"Scare me a little more, Maxie, and maybe I'll finish you quick." The raspy voice unnerved Maxie, but he was too arrogant to admit fear.

"Yeah, yeah. Listen, you choked up mug, I'm going enjoy watching ... oh!" With his throat closing and eyes twitching, fear now controlled Maxie as he looked up into the terrifying face of the Purple Scar!

Miles Murdock made his mask so frightful for two reasons: It accurately represented what his brother, police officer John Murdock, looked like when his scarred and mutilated body was pulled from the river last year. The combination of acid poured over his face and extended submersion in water left John looking like a nightmare. The dark purple also disappeared at night or in heavy shadow. More than one criminal never knew his death was at hand until he was close enough to look it in the eyes; as Maxie Smith did now.

"Anything you want, just ask! I work with the cops all the time, Scar! Capt. Griffin can tell you ...!"

"Quiet! One of my assistants recognized you and brought you here to answer my questions. Any other words from your mouth will not be tolerated." The macabre manhunter then walked behind him and turned on a grinding wheel to further unnerve the thug.

"My operative who saw you entering the Hot Spot remembered your face from the Devil's Thumb Incident last month. You were one of the few to escape me that night." The Purple Scar turned the hanging thug around to face him. "You won't be that lucky again." He picked up a large knife native to Palau and began sharpening the blade, paying careful attention to ensure the sparks struck Maxie in the face.

"When I'm done here, we'll start the questioning."

"You ain't got to do that, Scar! I'll tell you all about Parker working with those swells to take over the Westside."

"Swells?" The grim vigilante thought quickly and decided to follow Smith's offering. "So it's true that Parker has been trying to rise above his station in the gutter again?"

"He's got Hallick running a string of dirty cops on the Westside, Malcolm at the power company and that councilman from the 7th District to give it all a nice cover!"

"You mean Sinclair?" The Purple Scar demanded.

"Yeah, the guy all over the newspapers! He and the Boss are taking over the Westside along with the 7th to cut out a whole corner of Akelton."

The longest hour of Maxie's life passed in the basement of Miles Murdock's Down Street Free Clinic. The terrified thug eventually spilled the names of a dozen minor players along with Elliot Edgerton, manager of the largest bank in Akelton City. After that revelation, the masked avenger stepped out of the light to pick up a phone. Who he conferred with remained a mystery to the frightened thug.

"I guess I'm done with you, Maxie. Don't worry, this won't take long." Then he stepped back again into the darkness.

"No! I still got stuff to tell you, Scar! You ain't got to do this!"

Returning to Maxie's vision, the Purple Scar grabbed him by the back of his head and shoved an ether soaked rag over the thug's face with his free hand. The liquid from the rag spilled into his eyes, and the panicked thug screamed in terror believing the vigilante was blinding him with acid.

Maxie proved to be a wealth of knowledge about not just the conspiracy, but Dell Parker's entire organization in Akelton City's Westside. He was much higher up than just strong-arming merchants and other business owners, but the thug still had a twisted preference for getting his hands dirty.

What he didn't know was that the Purple Scar had Homicide Captain Dan Griffin standing by in the shadows, speaking to him while pretending to be on the phone. The big police officer had met Miles Murdock after his brother John joined the Akelton City Police Department and they had become friends almost immediately. John Murdock's murder two years before forged that friendship into a modern-day Damon and Pythias.

Even so, the police detective wouldn't condone the Purple Scar's more violent methods. When the masked vigilante contacted him, Captain Griffin agreed to an interrogation only if he could be there to keep his friend in check. Dan had no problems with knocking around a wife-beater or breaking arms to find a kidnapped child but torturing a helpless suspect for information was not in his bag of tricks regardless of how long he had known Miles and his late brother.

"What do you think?"

"I think this is way beyond anything Maxie used to give me when I was a Lieutenant." The big cop jerked his chin up at the mask. "Take that off and we can talk more."

Once he pulled off the mask, Miles Murdock began talking immediately. "I had no idea this was going on, Griff. I grabbed him thinking it was some run of the mill protection racket, but this is beyond anything I could have imagined."

"It doesn't make sense. Sinclair isn't even the councilman for the Westside district. That's Les Daniels. Parker is going to have to get rid of him for it to work."

"Unless Daniels is also part of it."

"I really doubt that, Miles. Daniels was elected four months ago, so he hasn't been in the political cesspool long enough to get infected yet. Keep in mind he got his start as a union organizer at Akelton Brickworks. He did such a good job there, the Westsiders elected him to the city council. He gives the Mayor regular heartburn and doesn't care much for those of us in blue. Sinclair's another case, though. He's an expert at keeping a public face but anyone with two bits' worth of sense knows he's a snake."

"The banker, Elliot Edgerton, has a personal reputation much like Sinclair. His business reputation, though, has always been scrupulously honest. I'm surprised his name is involved with this. I believe what we're seeing here is only half the plan, Griff."

Doc Murdock continued. "If you agree that Maxie has given us everything useful, we can get rid of him and work this out tomorrow. I don't have a lot of time before the ether begins to wear off, so what do you want to do with him?" Miles Murdock knew Dan wouldn't allow him to just end Maxie, no matter how much he might deserve it.

"He can still be useful to us later. I say we throw a blindfold on him, gag him and then you and Tommy dump him off on the edge of Dell Parker's territory once he starts to wake up."

The Doctor shook his head. "We can do that, but won't he run straight to his boss?"

"Not a chance. The last guy of Parker's we had in Police custody for more than a couple of hours was Mike Dodson. He disappeared right after we let him go. If Maxie lets slip that the Purple Scar grabbed him for even five minutes, he'll get the same treatment."

Griff slammed his fist into the doorframe hard enough to shake the floor. "I knew Parker had to have someone inside the Police to get Dodson eliminated that fast, but to hear it's a precinct lieutenant really digs in my guts. We're supposed to have the rats cleaned out before they get that big."

"We'll clean them out this time, Griff. I promise you that."

"Don't worry about it, Miles. When we get to that point, I'll take care of Hallick myself."

Suddenly concerned about his friend but needing to move on, the talented doctor changed the subject. "Do you need to take the car he was driving? There was something strange about how it handled and I'd like Tommy to look at it."

The homicide detective grinned ruefully. "That roadster of yours could probably use a break from the crashes and bullet holes. I'll take whatever is in it and check the license, make and model against the stolen vehicle report. You and Tommy use it to dump Maxie and then hide it until I get back with you. If it's not stolen; it's all yours."

"OK Dan. I'll have him look it over, and if he finds anything else interesting, I'll let you know immediately."

"Better hurry Miles. You're already late picking up Dale for dinner."

As Miles Murdock dropped his head and started groaning, Dan laughed and left him to his misery.

Tommy Pedlar's loyalty to Miles Murdock was as strong as the fear criminals had for the Purple Scar. Several years before creating his vigilante alter-ego, the talented plastic surgeon had restored the face of Tommy's daughter after she was horribly scarred in an auto accident.

It was when the bandages came off that the former second story man revealed his occupation to Miles Murdock and swore to him that he would not just fly straight from then on, but also promised to be at the doctor's beck and call for as long as he found Tommy useful. Since then, Tommy had proven himself very useful to both the Doctor and his grim alter-ego.

"Are you ready to go, Boss?"

"Yes, Tommy, but we'll need to hurry. I had to anesthetize Smith again before you arrived. Since Dan wants to keep him alive for later questioning, I want to avoid him seeing your face."

Once loaded, Tommy asked, "Where do you want to get rid of him?"

"We'll drop him in that empty lot just past Lee Street where it turns into 10th Avenue. Let's do that and then you can drop me off where I left the roadster."

Nurse Dale Jordan had worked with Doctor Murdock for the last three years after leaving her position at Akelton City General Hospital. The intelligent, highly skilled nurse helped him set up his free clinic on Down Street in Akelton City's poorest neighborhood, performed the duties of a surgical nurse there, as well as at the Swank Street Clinic, and oversaw the daily schedules for both practices. They had fallen in love shortly before the murder of his brother two years ago.

"You're late, Miles. When I called Doctor Everett an hour ago, he said you had left over an hour before that. Then Tommy runs out of here shouting about helping you. I hope it was a good enough reason to stand me up tonight; again!"

"Dale, I'm sorry; at first it just looked like Bill was in trouble but then this Maxie Smith began spilling everything and ..." Then he finally looked directly at her and noticed that her emerald eyes were dancing with mischief and not flashing with anger. "Oh very funny, young lady!"

The lithe, blonde woman laughed merrily. As she did, Miles Murdock felt the weight of his double life ease for just a moment. "Tommy explained everything. I'd apologize, Miles, but it's just too much fun to tweak your nose like a naughty little boy." She moved closer and put her hand on his chest.

"I must be getting used to this. When Tommy told me it was just one criminal you had gone after, I didn't even worry about it ..." She paused, "for about a minute anyway."

"Someday, Dale, I'll put this behind me." He pulled her into his arms. "I promise."

After a long embrace, she pulled back and looked up at her heart's desire. "I know, Darling, I know. For tonight though, I will happily settle for a now very late dinner and perhaps drinks. Tomorrow we'll talk about what you need to do and how Tommy and I can help."

"Anywhere except the Hot Spot and you've got a deal!"

As the couple left for their evening, Maxie Smith freed himself and began working his way down Lee Street, back to his apartment. Still stumbling from the effects of the ether and the sap, it took him over an hour to get home.

Despite that lingering confusion, he knew he had to come up with a story that would explain the missing car without Dell Parker killing him for losing it. Feeling the still swollen goose egg on his head, the thug decided to tell half the truth. He just needed a few more marks on his face.

Edward "Eddie" Pulaski had been the doorman at the Hapwell Arms for two years. He thought he had seen every kind of person come through the entrance, but tonight was the first time he saw someone who looked like they went through a buzz saw.

"Mr. Smith!" He ran to the door as Maxie fell against it, cracking his head against the glass, smearing blood from a wound on his forehead.

Pulling him inside, Eddie half-carried him to the elevator before Smith shuddered so hard he almost fell. Then the thug opened his eyes and grabbed Eddie's arm.

"Call Mr. Parker!" He croaked, "I got bad news, Eddie."

The next day, Tommy Pedlar had more questions than answers for his boss.

"Can Parker do this, Doc? Get such a grip on the Westside's medical care that people fall in line?"

"It's not only medical care, Tommy. Parker knows if he can get all of the basic services in a community under his control, then he has a virtual death grip on them. According to Dan Griffin, the only thing missing would be a way to keep the Mayor and the other city councilmen out of the way or make them a part of it."

"It's still only one corner of the city, Doc. It's not like this guy is going to be on an island and blow up all the bridges or something."

"Griff and I haven't figured that out yet, Tommy. Did you find out why the car handled so poorly?"

"Yeah, along with a few other surprises. The doors and quarter panels are all armored and the front end has been reinforced." He patted the car. "She'll knock over a fire hydrant, a street light or even a coupe like Dale's and keep going. There's an armor plate mounted behind the front seat, too. Someone tried to make this sedan into a Big Willie but still keep it looking like a Packard."

"What's screwy is that all of the glass is just normal thickness. No one's come up with a bullet proof windshield yet, but some glassmakers have gotten really good at windows thick enough to stop sledge hammers and small caliber ammunition. This windshield isn't that, though. It's like putting a guy in a suit of armor and then handing him a papier-mâché helmet."

The former Second-Story Kid motioned Miles Murdock towards the rear of the auto. "I also found some party favors in the trunk. It didn't look big enough, so I started checking for false panels." He opened what appeared to be the cover panel of the backseat. "Two Browning semi-automatics, four extra magazines, two Thompsons, four drum magazines and ..." He lifted the cover off what should have been the spare tire. "... enough .45 ammunition to invade Connecticut."

Murdock rubbed his chin thoughtfully. "So we've got a heavily armed Goliath that someone in the know can stop cold with a few well-aimed shots from a .38."

"That's about the size of it, Doc. Take out the driver and whoever's in the back is a sitting duck."

"That's more than interesting enough to call Griff."

Dan Griffin knew that nothing Maxie spilled about Parker could be used in court, but after a year of working with the Purple Scar, he had developed ways around that. He might direct an investigation by giving his "opinion" that would steer another detective in the right direction or tell a snitch where to go to find out the same information that could now be used to secure a warrant. Griff's methods were slower than the Purple Scar's, but they resulted in convictions and proved a lot less fatal for everyone involved.

He checked the information provided by Maxie Smith against current open cases and recent informant tips. After a thorough examination, he realized the brothel mentioned by Maxie as a meeting place for some of the conspirators would be a good, first domino to tip over in order to bring the whole thing down. The big cop quickly contacted the Vice Chief, Captain Bert Masterson, to give him a 'hot tip'.

"Tell you what, Bert, go in and tell your Precinct Captain the whole thing was your idea; take all the credit you want. I'm just after Parker's lieutenants. If you scoop any of them up, let me take them off your hands. Everyone else you grab in that raid is yours."

"What if we come up dry?"

"There's no chance of that, but if you do, I'll take the heat and Chalmers can tear me a new one."

"Deal! I can get the raid set up for tomorrow night, Dan. Do you want in on it?"

"No, let this go as an 'anonymous tip' for now. Like I said; if it falls apart on you, I'll take the heat."

+++

"I also found some party favors in the trunk."

"So that's everything up till now Miles, the raid is set. Bert Masterson is a straight arrow who hand-picked his squad over the last couple of years. If this goes off like Smith squealed, we should have at least one of Parker's lieutenants and a couple of the minor partners."

"That's good to know, Dan, especially considering what Tommy discovered with the car Maxie Smith was driving." He quickly detailed what Pedlar had found about the armor and weapons.

"There's no chance a crook like Dell Parker would send his people out in something like that or with that much firepower. I'll grab a uniform to run through all of the stolen vehicle reports until he finds something."

"That's a good idea. Now, what about the two names we already got from Smith?"

"Edgerton and Malcolm? I can't tie them to anything yet; maybe after the raid. Even if I get a warrant on a guy like Edgerton, his lawyer will just sit in front of him like a rooster guarding the hen house."

"Then maybe Edgerton needs an unofficial visit from a concerned citizen."

✝✝✝

Elliot Edgerton's business life was very regimented. He kept the same schedule, Monday through Friday, for the last two years since achieving his status as manager of the largest bank in Akelton City. This made finding him very easy for the Purple Scar; getting him not so much. Attacking at the bank was out of the question. It took the macabre manhunter only a moment to determine that assaulting Edgerton's home would be almost as difficult after seeing it. In-transit was the only option, which left him only a few minutes to plan.

Across the broad street from Edgerton's residence was another house, not yet completed, but with a finished driveway that was partially hidden from view. The Purple Scar quickly backed the sedan up the driveway and waited for his prey to approach. In a few minutes the car arrived, passing the hidden vigilante and stopping at the gated entrance. The driver called to the house and the gate began to open.

As the auto began moving again, the Purple Scar accelerated from the driveway, cut sharply left and struck the other vehicle across the rear tire, smashing the opposite side into the brick gatepost at a sharp angle. The armored auto crushed both rear quarter panels and broke the rear axle free of the undercarriage. The driver bounced off the steering wheel several times before finally collapsing on the front seat unconscious and bleeding.

The vigilante moved quickly from the sedan and looked through the shattered window. He found Edgerton lying on the backseat, stunned and clutching a sealed, cardboard box.

"Get up!" The Purple Scar growled at him and then dragged the banker from the wrecked automobile. "Move!" He pushed him toward the armored sedan.

The banker stopped, began shaking and stared at the other vehicle. "What did you do to Maxie Smith?"

The frightful vigilante stopped cold like someone had pole axed him. "You recognize this automobile?"

"It wasn't for you, it was for him." Edgerton's voice was barely above a whisper. Rousing slightly, he clutched the box tighter and began babbling.

Two men were running toward them from the house, guns already drawn. The Purple Scar drew his own; grabbed the banker by his collar and began dragging him to the other car.

The shorter thug yelled as they ran up and spread out. "Get away from the Scar, Mr. Edgerton. We'll put the freak put down!"

"Quiet, Edgerton!" The frightening vigilante dragged the banker in front of him. "Get in the car if you want to live through this!"

"Shut 'em both up, Carl!" The shorter thug yelled and then started shooting. BLAM! BLAM!

"Down!" The macabre manhunter pushed Edgerton to the ground behind the armored car and returned fire. BLAM! BLAM! Bullets ripped through his coat as he did, striking the taller gunman.

"I'm hit!" Carl yelped and started crawling to the cover of the wrecked auto.

The shorter gunman continued to fire at the Purple Scar and his hostage; trying to keep the scared banker from saying anything else. Other men began to emerge from the house; armed and running for the gunfight. Instead of waiting for them, he tried to move around the rear.

BANG! The Purple Scar was waiting and ended his life with one bullet through the right cheek and into the brain. In the next few seconds, the fearsome crime-fighter had Edgerton in the sedan and pulled away. He zigzagged to avoid the remaining thugs still throwing lead his direction. With the ruined automobile blocking the gate, no one would be coming after them.

"That's what Parker thinks of you Edgerton. Your men are under HIS orders to kill you in order to protect his own skin."

Edgerton was beyond hearing him though. "I wouldn't have talked," he gasped. "I wouldn't ..." His final words were finished in front of Saint Peter.

The Purple Scar reached over and pulled back the dead man's coat to find two bullet wounds. After driving another minute, he stopped the sedan and removed his mask. Miles Murdock pried the box from Edgerton's hands which rattled as he lifted it away. He removed the tape and opened the top, hoping for any answer to what was becoming an increasingly large knot of questions.

What he found were more questions and one-hundred recently pressed metal buttons that read 'Elect Edgerton'.

"So when are you going to drop off the body?" Griff was not happy, but he understood that there was very little the Purple Scar could have done once the bullets started flying.

Miles Murdock took a deep breath and pressed on. "I'd like to keep it on ice for now, Dan. If Parker doesn't know for certain that Edgerton is dead, then he may make additional mistakes."

"You're way out on a limb here, Miles. If that body is discovered, your entire world goes up in smoke."

"I'll take that risk."

"Have you told Dale and Tommy this is what you're doing?"

"I told Tommy last night and Dale when she came in earlier this morning."

"Get it done quickly, Miles."

"Okay, Dan. Look, I think the campaign buttons prove that Parker and Sinclair were going to replace Daniels with Edgerton. Do you know if he was the person supposed to receive the car?"

"Not sure. The uniform I've got digging into it hasn't found the car on any stolen vehicles lists and only one of the companies that build these autos has gotten back with me so far. Masterson should be making his raid in a couple of hours. I'll keep you posted if he nets any fish big enough to be useful."

+++

Later that night, Miles Murdock received his call.

"Bert picked up a hot one on the raid, Miles. He's here at the station now and we could use your help; get moving."

"I don't understand, Griff. Do you want me to follow a suspect after you release him?"

"No, we don't need the Scar. It's Miles Murdock that might get a confession out of this 'gentleman'." Griff said the last word with exaggeration and then started laughing. "Get down here and you'll figure it out."

Confused even further, the physician put down the phone and called Tommy on the intercom to get the roadster ready to go.

Doctor Murdock recognized Griff's prisoner immediately. Bernard Stampton-Wells was a member of the latest generation of one of Akelton City's upper crust families. Indolent and self-indulgent were the kindest words that could be applied to the fair-haired lay about. If his great grandfather could see him, the crooked gambler would have thrown his marked cards in the river in disgust.

As the arrogant socialite kept sparring with Griff, Miles Murdock realized that his friend was right; neither the police nor the Purple Scar would get him to confess even that the sky is blue. Someone else, though, could certainly force him to cooperate by threatening the only thing a man like Bernard value, his standing in high society. He tapped on the glass to alert Dan he was there and then waited for him.

Bernard looked up as Griff walked back in, but noticed he left the door open.

"Bringing out the really big rubber hoses this time Captain?"

"No, Bernie, I'm going to introduce one of our advisors to the police department and let him work you over." Griff shouted over his shoulder and out the door. "Hey, Doc! Come on in!"

Miles Murdock walked in with a large smile on his face. "Bernard Atticus Stampton-Wells. How are you, old boy?"

The sneer left the socialite's face the moment he saw the Doctor. "What are you doing here, Miles?"

"It's exactly what Captain Griffin said. The police call me to consult if there is a medical aspect to a crime or if they have a prisoner that may need medical attention." He pointed at Bernard's left arm. "One of the officers who brought you in noticed you were favoring that arm. They didn't re-injure that old auto racing injury did they? The one in Virginia."

It was common knowledge in Akelton's high society that Stampton-Wells broke his arm falling out of a window while escaping a jealous husband. Making up a story to avoid personal embarrassment in front of the 'common people' put Bernard on Miles Murdock's side immediately.

"Oh I'm fine, Miles. It was never properly set so I get an ache when the weather's too damp. I should start wintering in Florida."

"You should; the scenery is certainly better in January than it is here." Both men laughed at that, then Miles motioned him closer. "I've seen this Captain Griffin work before. He knows how things are around here, but he's going to want some little tidbit to feed his ego before he cuts you loose."

"Cooperate with the police, Miles? That's like having tea with the chauffeur and I won't do it." Bernard leaned back in his chair.

"Oh come on, Bernard! There are cathouses all across Akelton. Surely the one they caught you in can't be that good." He tapped his fingers on the table. "What exactly does Griffin want anyway?"

"After they picked us up, one of the doxies let slip I was there last week on the same night. Captain Flatfoot wants to know who I saw and what time I saw them."

"Then you may be the one with the advantage, Bernard."

"How do you come to that conclusion, Miles?" He shook his handcuffs at the doctor. "It doesn't feel that way to me."

"Captain Griffin works Homicide, not Vice. That's higher up their chain of command I guess you could call it. If he's looking for someone, then it has nothing to do with you except as a witness. If you confirm what he suspects, then he has the power to make all this disappear. He might even have a patrolman swear you were with the Salvation Army tonight feeding the hungry."

The socialite smiled and slapped his hand on the table. "I like that, Miles! Let's get Captain Flatfoot back in here and get started!"

+++

"You were responsible for that car, Maxie. Not only did you lose it, but the Scar somehow got his hands on it and used it to take out Edgerton."

"But, Boss, I'm telling you the car was stolen from my apartment building! I drove directly there after I left the Hot Spot!"

"The hat check girl said someone else drove off in the sedan, Maxie. She saw it clearly from the kitchen entrance as the car drove by the alley."

"That dame's got it in for me Mr. Parker! She's just mad 'cause I roughed her up a little for knocking over the coat rack!"

"There's no need to shout, Maxie." Dell Parker liked to think of himself as a reasonable man. Reasonable men rarely found the need to shout and expected everyone around them to behave accordingly.

"Sorry, Boss."

"Your building is only fifteen minutes from the Hot Spot. Why did it take you over three hours to crawl through the front door after you left?"

"I got cracked in the head, Boss. I must've been laying outside the building for a couple of hours."

Parker shook his head. "There was someone outside the Arms before you made a scene Maxie. No one saw you."

"Whoever said that is a dirty liar Boss. I'll kill him for that."

Parker nodded to a man behind Maxie. "Well, Edward, who's telling the truth?"

"I am, Sir. I make regular patrols around the building. It keeps the cops away or at least out of sight. I was outside just before Mr. Smith stumbled into the Hapwell a little after ten o'clock."

Dell stopped any argument with a wave. "Edward works for me, Maxie. Being the doorman at your apartment building is only secondary. His primary job is to keep track of everyone at the Hapwell; which I own by the way, who works for me."

The crime boss walked around his desk and up to Maxie. "So you see there's no hope of leaving here on your own feet unless you tell me the complete truth. If I like what you say, you get to go, and all is forgiven. The worst thing that will happen is you won't feel the end coming. However, if you lie again, I'll make sure you die screaming."

Maxie started nodding fast. "You got it, Mr. Parker. Nothing but the truth, I swear it."

The younger thug kept his word and so did Dell Parker. Maxie never felt it.

"Someone call Hallick. I have something for him to do."

+++

"Dan Griffin is on the phone, Miles. He doesn't sound happy to be calling either."

"Thank you, Dale." He picked up the extension. "Hello, Griff. Did Bernard provide anything that paid off?"

"He did. The list of other clients at the cathouse that night matched up with two of the names we got from Maxie. The guy Bernie recognized but couldn't name turned out to be the utilities manager, Steven Malcolm. That gave us just enough detail for a search warrant on Malcolm's properties; the charges are 'moral turpitude' and 'consorting with prostitutes'."

Griff continued. "It's being served in an hour. If we find anything at all tying him to Maxie or Dell Parker, we can roll them all up for questioning. If no one talks, I can't hold them for more than twenty-four hours, but that should be enough to throw a wrench into their plans."

"Which should give us enough time to finish off this conspiracy. That's excellent news, Griff! You don't sound happy though."

"Because that's not all of it, Miles. That sedan you picked up? It was supposed to be delivered to Councilman Sinclair's office."

"Sinclair?!"

"That's right. It was converted by the Standard Arms and Armor Company. According to them, they had installed bullet resistant glass in the windshield, rear window and in all the doors."

"So Parker had it grabbed and the window glass switched out?"

"That's it, Miles. If you hadn't snatched Maxie, Councilman Sinclair would be riding around in that sedan right now."

"So Parker has been planning a double-cross for Sinclair."

"That's still not the end of it Miles. Maxie Smith just turned up in the city morgue along with a 'John Doe'. When we get him identified, I'm certain he'll turn out to be the missing Standard driver who was supposed to deliver the armored auto to Councilman Sinclair. Either someone saw you toss him out of the car, or Parker decided to tie up loose ends once the auto went missing."

"Then Parker knows that the Purple Scar is after him."

"I wouldn't bet against it, Miles. Parker is as smart as they come when it comes to gang bosses."

Miles Murdock thought about it for a moment. "Sinclair is most likely still ignorant of Parker's plan to double-cross him. If we confront the councilman, it may be our chance to turn him against his other partners. Perhaps make him think that Parker still sees a chance to get rid of him and then frame him to make the public think Sinclair was the mastermind."

"It's a great idea, Miles." Griff chuckled. "Do you know anyone that could pull that off? I'd do it, but I'm riding along to serve the warrant on Evan Malcolm tonight."

"Not to worry, Dan, I know someone that can handle it for us."

As the two men spoke, William Everett was making notes from his last patient. When he heard the front door open again, he didn't even look up. "I'll be out in a minute!" He walked out from the examination room to find his patients gone and three white men instead waiting for him.

"Good evening, Doctor. My name is Dell Parker and I'd like to talk to you about one of my employees."

William Everett looked around as the other two men began looking through his appointment book and receipts. "Who is it you think I know about Mr. Parker?"

"Maxie Smith. He came by here yesterday to speak with you about business insurance and a possible job offer."

"He was here. I turned him down."

"I'm disappointed of course, but that's not something I'm concerned about right now, Doctor. Maxie has disappeared and I'm concerned for him."

"He was fine when he left here, Mr. Parker."

"I know he was, Doctor; oh, wait, it's not doctor yet is it?" The gang boss sat down. "Anyway, he arrived at the Hot Spot when he was supposed to. What I need to know is who was here that may have seen Maxie."

"I was already done seeing patients before Maxie arrived. That's probably why he came by as late as he did."

"Was there anyone here that wasn't a patient?"

The man with the appointment book approached Parker. "I got something here, Boss. A set of initials that show up whenever the Doc here is stitching people up and stuff like that. He's checked off on nearly everything that day and he was here right before Maxie showed up."

Parker looked over at the book. "M.M.? Who's that, William?"

"That would be Doctor Miles Murdock. Until I'm licensed, he's on my shoulder like a guardian angel." The young doctor wanted to tell them nothing, but remembered that Doctor Murdock had signed for supplies that day as well. His name would be found in another minute.

"So he was here when Maxie showed up?"

After hesitating for a moment, William realized that they were going to visit Doctor Murdock next no matter what he said. "Yes, but he was in the back getting washed up to leave. They never saw each other."

"Did you tell him anything?"

"No, he heard the door close as he walked out of the washroom, but I told him it was just another patient; no names."

"You didn't complain or ask for his help?"

"Never crossed my mind. No rich, white doctor is going to put his neck out for someone from the Westside. I'm just his latest charity project."

Parker got up to leave. "Well that's true enough. Just a couple more things to do and we'll be on our way."

Dale burst into the doctor's office. "Miles, Dr. Everett is on the phone! He says it's an emergency."

Grabbing the extension, he asked, "Bill? What's happened?"

"This is a heads up call, Doctor. Dell Parker just paid me a visit. He's claiming that Maxie Smith disappeared and he's worried about him, so he's tracing his boy's steps."

"Are you all right? What about the clinic?"

"I'm fine, but every drug and medical supply worth taking, they took. Parker's way of making a point I guess. While he was trying to talk nice, one of his people went through the appointment calendar and figured out you were here when Maxie came by. I told them you just heard the door close and it was simply another patient; no names or details. I think they believed me, but Parker and some of his boys are heading for your clinic next."

The doctor buzzed for Dale to come back in the office and began writing. "Were they coming directly here from your office?"

"I don't think so, one of Parker's people mentioned picking someone up on the way, but that could have been a lie for me."

Dale walked in the office. Miles Murdock held up a note: 'Trouble coming, call Tommy and go'. The blonde beauty looked at him with disdain and shook her head no.

"How long since they left?"

"Five minutes. I made sure they were gone and then went out the back and down the alley. They tore out the clinic's phone so I'm using the one at the dry cleaners the next street over."

"That was smart, Bill. Let's see, if Parker doesn't stop, he and his people will be here in ten minutes."

"Just disappear for a couple of days!"

"If I do that they'll be convinced I was involved. Don't worry Bill, I've dealt with these people through my free clinic every week. Someone is always coming around trying to extort money."

"I hate to even ask Doctor, but do you know what happened to Smith?"

"No, Bill. The last time I saw him, Maxie Smith was alive and perfectly healthy."

Parker and his gangsters arrived at the Swank Street Clinic twenty minutes later, with another person. Miles had already positioned himself in the reception area, looking like he was ready to leave. Dale and Tommy were in one of the examination rooms for safety but only after Dale loudly protested. Both were armed.

"Good evening, Doctor; my name is Dell Parker. I'd like to talk to you about one of my employees."

"Is he a patient here? I can't give you any medical information."

"No, Doctor. I just need to know if you met one of my people, Maxie Smith. It would have been this week at William Everett's clinic over on the Westside."

"Can't say as I have. I do know the name from the newspapers though. You say he works for you?"

The gang boss' face twitched but he held onto his smile. "I should have said he used to work for me, yes." Parker turned back to look at the coat-check girl from the Hot Spot. "Do you recognize the good doctor, Evelyn?"

"No, Mr. Parker. That guy was about as plain as a glass of milk." She looked Miles Murdock up and down. "No one is ever gonna say that about this tall drink of bourbon and water." She smiled and winked. "How 'bout it, Doc? You busy tomorrow night?"

"My schedule is pretty full, Evelyn; thank you for asking, though."

"It never hurts a girl to ask Handsome."

Parker stared at the tall doctor for another moment and then got up from his chair. "I guess that's it for now. Sorry to have bothered you, Doctor. Pick your chin up off the floor, Evelyn, and let's go."

"How 'bout it, Doc? You busy tomorrow night?"

"'Bye, Handsome. See you soon if you're smart." She blew him a kiss on the way out.

Dale walked in after they drove off. "If that little tramp called you 'Handsome' one more time, I was going to come out and shoot her anyway."

"Everything is fine, Dale. I'm certain Parker had her flirt just to see my reaction." Then he saw Tommy behind her giving him an 'ixnay' signal and changed the subject.

"They had someone going through your desk and filing cabinet while Parker and I spoke, would you please see if anything is missing?"

Dale walked to the file cabinet, muttering about ripping out hair by the roots if her files were disturbed.

"Boss, do you think you should call Captain Griffin and let him know Parker came by?" Miles Murdock didn't respond. "Doc?"

"What? Oh, sorry, Tommy; look at that mirror across from the window and tell me what you see."

"I see the mirror and the window it's reflecting, Boss."

"What else is in the reflection?"

Confused, Tommy began listing what he saw. "The curtains Dale put up last Thanksgiving, the building across the street and a car in front of the building."

Miles Murdock nodded. "That car pulled up along with Dell Parker. Whoever is inside is waiting for us to make a move. Let's not disappoint them."

"Fill me in, Doc. I'm still confused."

"We're going to pretend Dale and I are taking the roadster out for a drive. You hide in the back and then we'll switch while changing a tire. The two of you continue while I sneak back here and take the sedan to confront Sinclair."

Tommy nodded his head. "OK, I get it now. You better take Dale's car, though. Unless you're planning to crash again, the sedan is still looking pretty bad after grabbing Edgerton."

"Good idea, Tommy. Tell Dale to grab her coat and then get the roadster ready to go. I'll call Griff and then meet you two in the garage."

Once they departed the clinic, Doctor Murdock made certain to drive by the waiting car slow enough to be certain they saw him, but not so slow (he hoped) to arouse suspicion. After making sure they followed, he left the dense city center and headed for Akelton City Park.

About a minute after entering the park, he pulled over on a low rise. An approaching auto could not see the right side. He quickly got out, removed the jack and spare tire and then made a show of removing his hat and coat and throwing them in the back seat next to a hidden Tommy. Dale held a flashlight while he changed the tire.

"AHHHH!" The men in the other car jumped when Miles Murdock cried out, pretending to have hurt his hand while lowering the car. As they looked on, he threw the tire and jack in the trunk while whispering for Tommy to put on his hat and coat and slide out of the back seat to crouch on the ground. Dale turned off the flashlight and neither thug could see the switch in the dark.

Continuing the charade, Dale slid over to drive while Tommy tried to sit up as tall as he could. Without looking at him, she whispered, "Be careful Miles". He simply smiled at her, nodded and slid down the embankment. Then Tommy closed the door and they drove off. Fifteen minutes later, the Purple Scar was in Dale's coupe and driving to Sinclair's home.

"Glad you could join us, Captain."

"Thanks for letting me in on this warrant, Bert."

Masterson grinned. "After handing me that raid, I'll let you join my family for every Sunday dinner this year. The arrests alone look good, but that list of clients is going to let us turn informants in nearly every crooked pie in the city."

"Good to hear." Griff looked at the house. "Any movement?"

"No; nothing in the windows, no servants coming out asking us for ID to show the homeowner."

"Heh! I once had a butler ask me to place my badge on a silver tray so he could present it to the 'mahster of the house'. I told him to put the tray down or I'd cuff him to the 'mahster' and take them both in."

The Vice lieutenant laughed and checked his personal weapon. "Ready to go in?"

"Yeah, let's get him."

Masterson motioned to the rest of the arresting team and they moved to the front door. Two men were already in place covering the back of the house. Captain Griffin held back and watched them enter. Once they were all inside, he entered the house carefully, not wanting to interfere. They moved quickly through the empty house, checking rooms and finally arriving at Malcolm's study.

"Cap! You better come see this."

Griff entered the room to find Malcolm behind his desk, a pistol on the desktop and blood and brains on the back of the chair and the wall behind him.

"They can't all be winners, Captain."

"I still feel like they get away sometimes and I'm not certain this was a suicide, Bert."

"Looks pretty clear to me."

"Malcolm was a big player and had ties to old money. Men like that don't check themselves out until after they're found guilty and don't want to face the sentence."

"Lieutenant?" One of the sergeants watching the back walked into the study. "There's a trash barrel filled with ashes on the patio."

"Was he burning dirty pictures?"

"Don't know yet, Sir. A few bits look like blueprints of some sort. The barrel's still warm though."

Griff jumped in. "Is it warmer than Malcolm here?"

The sergeant blanched, but went over and touched the left hand of the corpse. "He's colder than the barrel, Captain."

"It's not exactly scientific Bert but it sure looks like Malcolm killed himself before he lit the fire in that barrel."

"Hell's Bells!"

"My feelings exactly, Bert." Griff looked over at the clock. There was no way of getting hold of Miles Murdock, but Tommy and Dale might be near the phone.

"Bert, can you keep an eye on this? I'm going to the nearest pay phone to call in my boys so I don't put down any fingerprints here."

"Yeah, Captain, we'll take care of it."

After Maxie and the Standard Driver turned up dead, Dan Griffin knew he'd have to personally face Hallick and his crooked cops. Both bodies had been hosed down and dressed in old clothes with no tags or laundry marks. If the uniformed officer who found them hadn't been in on an arrest of Smith two years ago, they might not have been identified for another week.

The phony suicide was nearly perfect as well, Dan thought. The killer was smart and made sure the coroner would have very little to work with there as well. Hallick was going to have to be brought down hard; hard enough that no cop was even going to think about getting crooked for a long time.

Seeing a phone booth, Dan pulled over and got out to call in a team from his Homicide Division. When two cars moved in to block him, he realized that moment was now.

"Hello Captain."

"Ben Hallick. I was just thinking about you." He cocked his head at the sound of men moving behind him. "Your boys move like a herd of hippos. Someone needs to teach them about approaching a suspect quietly."

"You aren't a suspect, Captain Griffin, just another mugging victim. The beat cop who finds you will think a couple of bums rolled you and then panicked when they figured you were a cop and tried to cover their tracks by killing you."

" 'Tried' to cover their tracks?"

"Well of course we're going to find who did this to you. There are always a couple of drunks around town that need to be put out of their misery anyway." Unknown to Hallick, his choice of words sealed his fate with Dan Griffin.

"So shooting me is out of the question?"

"Not unless I have to. Drop the .38." He shrugged when Griff hesitated. "It's your last chance to get in a few licks Captain. Might as well go along with it."

"I'm guessing you want the .32 in my coat pocket as well?"

"We'll take that pocketknife too. Pat him down McInary."

A weasel looking detective searched Dan quickly, taking the two pistols and the pocketknife. He tossed them onto the back seat of the sedan they drove up in.

"You sure that's it McInary?"

"Yeah, Lieutenant. The Captain here's a Boy Scout. Doesn't even want to carry a sap." The dirty cop sneered at Griff when he said it.

"Give him the full Broderick boys. I have an appointment to make."

"Hallick." He turned back to face Griff. "Leave town now. When I'm done here, I'm coming for you. It won't be to arrest you now either."

Hallick just smiled, got in his unmarked prowler and drove off.

The moment the car turned the corner, Griff was on McInary in two steps. A single punch laid the mouthy cop out cold on the sidewalk, but before he hit the concrete; the big man was already moving to the second dirty cop with a grim smile.

"I don't carry a sap because I don't need one. Let's get to it, you wannabe droppers; I got a promise to keep."

The other two, realizing they had lost the bulge in this fight, spread out and tried to squeeze Griff between them. With neither one drawing a weapon, he already had a plan.

"Come on!" He roared and charged the one to his left. Griff faked a punch and then kicked him hard in the knee. The supposed hard man went down like a puppet with its strings cut. The last cop grabbed him around the neck like he had hoped instead of getting punched in the kidneys.

Griff reached back, grabbed his opponent by the right ear and began pulling him around and forward. Now the dirty cop had a choice of either loosening his arm around his throat or have the big Captain tear his ear off. Distracted by the pain, he failed to see Griff's other hand reach back and gouge his right eye.

"GAAAAHHHH!" He let go and tried to cover his face. Griff dropped the man hard to the street with a haymaker.

The last man limped for the sedan. He got the suicide door opened and his hand on Griff's .38 just as the Homicide Captain crashed into it. The heavy door pinned the other man's legs and fractured his cheekbone against the frame. Then Griff pulled back the door and ripped the weapon from the younger cop's hand, breaking his trigger finger. As he slid to the ground, Dan slapped him hard on the side of his head for good measure.

"Where is Hallick going? Come on, you're heading to jail, make sure the chief weasel gets his."

He stared up at the Homicide Captain. "You really gonna settle accounts?"

Griff nodded. "He killed a man who was supposed to be in police custody and planned to murder two more just to cover his own tail. I won't let that slide, even for a cheap thug like Dodson and a couple of boozehounds."

"Hot Spot. He's meeting with Parker at the Hot Spot."

A few minutes later, Griff was able to get ahead of Hallick and cut him off three blocks from the club by crashing McInary's sedan into the smaller prowl car. The force of the crash threw the Lieutenant across the front seat and partially through the passenger window. Broken glass tore into him, collapsing a lung and shredding his insides.

Dan slowly got out of the wrecked sedan; ribs sore, shoulder dislocated and head bleeding from striking the steering wheel. He stumbled over to Hallick and pulled him out of the car to the ground.

He wheezed and choked on his own blood, but the dying lieutenant still grinned at Griff. "I guess you kept that promise after all. I should've tried to get you to come in with us."

"Never happen you little rat. I've bent the rules, but I never killed a man without cause."

"Big words coming from you, Dan. You just have someone else pull the trigger."

"What's that supposed to mean?"

"I'm not the only one who's figured out you're working with the Purple Scar." He wheezed again, this time spitting blood. "I told Parker to wait until we figured out who that freak really is; then we get rid of both of you."

"Good thing for me he didn't listen."

"Yeah, I should have thrown in with Sinclair ... Cough Cough! How are you going to hide this one? It's too big to sweep."

Griff just shook his head. "There's the real difference between you and me. Someday I'll answer for working off the books, but getting rid of you I'm writing in big red letters."

He leaned into the dying man's face. "I'm not running to some mob boss like a scared little daisy."

"Brave talk now Boy Scout. We'll see if you're that brave when ... COUGH COUGH!" Whatever he was going to say, died on his lips.

Griff turned at the sound of approaching sirens and pulled his badge out of his pants pocket. Fortunately, he knew the uniformed sergeant behind the wheel. The rookie with him just stared in confusion.

"Good evening Sergeant Brewer! How would you like to make Detective Third Grade tonight?"

"Is that Lieutenant Hallick on the ground Captain?"

"That's 'former Lieutenant' Hallick and yes, it certainly is. You'll find more of his fellow rats cuffed together over on Fourth near Albertson." The big cop noticed the whip antenna on the police vehicle. "Can you call that in for me?"

Brewer looked over his shoulder. "Snart! Call it in and be sure to let everyone know that Captain Griffin says they aren't us anymore." He turned back to Griff. "Is that about right Sir?"

"That's it exactly, Detective Brewer. Also, send a Homicide team out to Steven Malcolm's house. Lieutenant Masterson from Vice is already out there waiting for them "

"Go ahead then, lad." The rookie got back in the radio car to call it in.

"I'd also like to borrow Snart and your radio car to drive me to the hospital once I make a call. You'll be busy controlling the area and getting promises of free beer on your new promotion."

"Certainly, Captain!"

Despite the blood dripping off his skull and left arm hanging useless, Griff smiled as he entered a nearby phone booth and called the Swank Street Clinic. Tommy answered before the second ring.

"Boss?"

"No, Tommy, it's Dan Griffin. Tell Miles that we found Steven Malcolm already dead and he doesn't have to worry about Hallick. I've taken care of him and most of his bully boys. The scrubs are going to jail and their washerwoman boss won't be writing anymore parking tickets; ever. I'm not going to be able to help him wrap up Parker, though. If he wants to try to catch the last of the rats tonight, they're supposed to be meeting at the Hot Spot."

"Do you need anything, Captain? I can come down and bring you here. Dale is on the way now if you need patching up."

"No, I have a very nervous uniform waiting to take me to Akelton City General; he's already convinced I'm going to die before we get there. Besides, with what I'm sure Miles has planned, he'll need you both. One last thing Tommy."

"Yes Captain Griffin?"

"If you see the Purple Scar tonight, tell him I said, 'Good Hunting'."

Councilman Matthew Sinclair's home was not the fortress that Eliot Edgerton lived in. It was still big enough though for servants and a separate entrance for deliveries. After stepping over a low wall, the Purple Scar quickly moved across the side yard and picked the cheap lock on the servant's entrance.

Finding no one on the first floor, the vigilante moved upstairs and started checking doors. A voice called out from the master bedroom. "If you're here to kill me, come inside and we can discuss this like civilized men."

"Griff...called the Swank Street Clinic."

The macabre manhunter pushed in the door and then carefully entered the bedroom with his .38 pointed ahead. Sinclair was standing by a writing desk with his hands up and empty.

"You must be the Purple Scar. Dell Parker talks about you all the time. Care for a scotch?"

"I have better taste in who I drink with."

"Yes, I'm certain you think so."

"The conspiracy is over, Sinclair. You don't seem surprised, though."

"I knew it was a risk, but the reward would have been worth it."

"How did all of this get started?"

"It was the election of that rabble rouser Les Daniels. His last fight as a union boss nearly crippled Steven Malcolm financially. His desire to take back what Malcolm thought belonged to him eventually led us to my business associate Dell Parker. Once we all sat down to look at it, both of them got greedy and decided to take over the Westside for themselves. I saw it as a way to consolidate political power and eventually more."

"So the plan was to have Daniels die spectacularly and then his district folds into yours? That wouldn't let you undo anything he had accomplished before getting elected."

"His death was only the beginning. Malcolm already knew where the weaknesses are in the sewer and gas systems under most of Akelton City. In another week, we would have executed our plans to trigger a series of gas explosions in the Westside and frame Daniels for it."

"After the police found information we were going to plant at his home, my man at the Times would have smeared Daniels as the mastermind of Akelton's underworld. Half of the city already suspects him of being crooked just because of his union ties; our evidence would have convinced the city council to void every agreement he helped forge over the last year."

"You would have been a King for only a couple of months before a special election was held, Sinclair. Whatever power you had would disappear in a few weeks after that. You were going to murder hundreds of people just for that?"

Sinclair slapped the desktop and snarled at him. "Don't you understand yet? That's more than enough time for what I needed! Only fools like Parker and Malcolm would think we could take over an entire corner of Akelton City. It's the cash that flows into a city after such a disaster that makes it worth the effort! Even just a month of stealing the entire budget for two districts would have put more money into my pockets than six months of working behind the scenes with that idiot Dell Parker."

"I'm guessing all of that funding flows right through Edgerton's bank."

Sinclair laughed and then continued. "Add in all the emergency funds and charity dollars that pour in after a disaster like this and by the end of next month, I would have been in Central America with enough money to buy my own country."

The grim avenger shook his head. "It never would have happened, Sinclair. I intercepted the armored car that was supposed to be delivered to you. Parker had the special glass replaced with ordinary thickness in the windshield and doors. There was even a hidden compartment full of guns to ruin your reputation."

He continued, moving closer to the crooked politician. "When I tried to confront Edgerton about his role in all this, I discovered a box of these." He removed one of the election badges from his coat and threw it at Sinclair. "Parker already had a replacement picked out. If it weren't for me, his double-cross might have already ended your life."

Mistaking the Purple Scar's revelation for interest, Sinclair continued. "Join me then! You can eliminate Parker and have his slice of the pie. You'll be richer than your wildest dreams."

"There's your problem, Sinclair. I only dream of vengeance." BLAM!

The corrupt politician had made his choice which allowed the Purple Scar to hand out final justice. Final Judgment was now being passed by a higher power. He was certain he would have only had a short time before someone discovered Sinclair's body and reported it back to Dell Parker. There was still time to rifle his office, though. Once done, he called Tommy Pedlar.

"Sinclair is finished. There's a steel box with a combination, about the size of a suitcase. Can you talk me through opening it?"

"You're no can opener Boss, drag it home and I'll get it in two shakes. Before you hang up though, Captain Griffin called."

"Did he have anything else useful?"

"Better than that. He got jumped by that dirty button Hallick and a few of his boys, but turned the tables on them. Malcolm is already dead, but he told me that Parker and the last of the rats are meeting at the Hot Spot if you want to try to finish this tonight."

"Anything else?"

"No, but Captain Griffin was pretty banged up. He was headin' for the hospital once he got off the horn."

"You sound worried about him, Tommy."

"I think he's hoping the last of those dirty buttons will be at The Hot

Spot. He said something I thought I'd never hear coming out of a straight arrow kind of guy like that."

"What did he say?"

"He said to tell the Purple Scar, 'Good Hunting'."

The macabre manhunter thought quickly. "Tommy, we're going to need the sedan we confiscated from Maxie Smith again."

"She still looks bad, Boss, but she runs. It's in a storage unit right near the Swank Street clinic."

"Meet me two blocks up from The Hot Spot. I'm going to need the sedan and the equipment you found in the trunk. Dell Parker has insulated himself from the law, so I'm going to deliver justice on him personally."

"You got it Boss. I'll be there in ten minutes."

"Faster, Tommy. Once they find out Sinclair is dead, the rest of the key players in this won't be there for long."

Nine minutes later, the Purple Scar pulled up behind Tommy and the sedan. The former second-story kid was standing by the open trunk. He had already loaded one of the drum magazines and inserted it into a Thompson. He had rigged both of them with a sling since the last time the vigilante saw them.

"What's the plan, Boss?"

The Purple Scar took the Thompson from Pedlar and pulled back the action, chambering a round. Then he added the .45s to his coat pockets. "I go in and kill every one of them. These miserable excuses for men tried to turn the Westside of Akelton City into their personal fiefdom. I'm going to drag them out of the Middle Ages and into Hell."

Tommy shivered a bit but bravely asked, "What else can I do?"

"I need a very loud distraction."

As the sedan passed the alleyway entrance, the macabre vigilante kicked in the kitchen entrance door. By the time the front doors and windows shattered, he had already moved quickly through the kitchen and into the dining room. The foot soldiers and bodyguards had just begun shooting at the auto when the Purple Scar stepped behind them and pulled the trigger.

RAT-A-TAT-TAT!!!! The Thompson spat lead into the conspiracy members and their gunmen, killing most and keeping the rest down while Tommy slid out of the driver's door and then low-crawled through the remains of the club's entrance to wait for the police to respond to the sound of gunfire. Death, however, did not wait for anyone else.

The Purple Scar tossed the now empty Thompson on the bar and swung the second one up to bear. After firing two short bursts at rapidly overturned tables, he moved closer to make sure no one escaped this time. Four more bursts finished off the gunmen, leaving the gang boss alone and bleeding behind the bar.

"Your day is over, Parker! Sinclair is dead and his papers are in the hands of the police. Step out now and I'll give you a cleaner death than you deserve."

"I'll wait for the cops you freak!"

"Wrong choice! Your pet lieutenant is already dead and half of his dirty cops are in handcuffs. I'm guessing the rest of them are dead on the floor here."

"I can pay! There's enough here in the club ..." BRAAAAAP!!!!! Chunks and splinters from the reinforced table flew through the air. Glassware and bottles shattered, spilling their contents everywhere.

"Wrong move Parker! Sinclair already offered me your cut for his life and I punched his ticket. Same offer holds; stand up and it'll be quick."

"Scar!"

He turned at Tommy's voice, just in time to dodge gunfire from a late arrival. The shots ripped through his coat and grazed his side, with one round drilling a bloody hole through his right thigh.

Thinking the Purple Scar was down, the last of Hallick's cops swung around to draw a bead on Tommy. That was his final mistake. The gruesome vigilante flipped onto his back, pulled one of the .45s from his coat and emptied half the magazine into the spine of the crooked cop.

"NNGGHH!" The Purple Scar levered himself up on his uninjured leg; just in time to see Dell Parker rise from behind the bar. Two shots from the .45 put him back down while the wounded sentinel jumped closer to the table.

Stopping fifteen feet away, he realized how much alcohol was spilled behind the bar. The same contents the now former gang boss was covered in. The Purple Scar quickly reached down and jammed a napkin into a half-full bottle near his feet then pulled out his lighter.

Parker called out. "Last chance, Scar. You walk out, I walk out. We can always dance next week."

"You're too scared to run now aren't you, Parker?" He rasped. "You stopped calling me freak." Lighting the napkin, he lobbed it just over the bar to shatter next to the criminal. "Here's some incentive!"

"AAAHHHHH!!" Hair and coat on fire, Parker began to run for the exit.

BLAM! BLAM! The Purple Scar's .45 spat lead into the back of Parker's skull, killing him instantly and giving Parker the same death he had promised Maxie Smith.

"Boss!"

"Is anyone else out there?"

"No, everyone else was smart enough to run and hide." Tommy approached the Purple Scar carefully. "Let's get out of here before someone gets more curious than scared."

"All right, Tommy ... No wait!"

"Boss we gotta go!" Pedlar insisted.

"One quick stop in the back office, Tommy, and then you can get me to the Swank Street clinic fast as you can. I know Dale's waiting and from now on, I'm not going to complain about it."

Pedlar was able to pull the heavily damaged sedan out of the club and nurse it back to the roadster. They switched cars and he quickly got his boss back to the Swank Street clinic; using side streets and the police radio concealed in the roadster to avoid responding patrol units. Once inside, Dale Jordan took over. She immediately determined that she could deal with the bullet wound and dismissed Tommy.

"You're sure I can't help, Dale?"

"Yes, Tommy. Go clean up the car or put away the guns."

Doctor Murdock tried to rise on one elbow. "There's that safe and the ..."

Dale turned on him, eyes blazing. "Lie back and be quiet, Miles, or I swear I'll put a matching bullet hole in the other leg."

Tommy began backing out of the exam room. "I'll go and open that can, Dale. By tomorrow, the roadster will be clean as a whistle."

"How's the leg, Dear?"

"I'll let you know when the pain medication wears off. Any chance of getting breakfast?"

"You mean dinner. I closed up the clinic here and Doctor Kiley was already signed up to volunteer at the free clinic today anyway."

"Dinner? How much morphine did you give me?"

"Obviously it was enough to keep you unconscious until dinner time; just like I planned."

"Is this like the time you tried to cook Chinese? I should just be quiet and smile?"

Dale ignored the jab completely. "You're going to love what Tommy found in that portable safe. I know Doctor Everett certainly will."

Several days later, Dan Griffin invited the Medical Recommendation Board to a meeting in their own conference room at Akelton City General. The reason given was that it had to do with the recent bloodshed and arrests from last week. Each man around the table had a dozen questions but the look on Captain Griffin's face kept them quiet.

"Thank you, gentlemen, for coming in on short notice. Before anyone asks about Dr. Lochner, your former head of the board has resigned and will be on the Silver Express leaving town this evening." He gestured to the far side of the conference room.

"As most of you know, Dr. Murdock works with us when the Police Department has a case requiring medical knowledge. I'll let him explain further."

"Thank you, Captain Griffin. With Dr. Lochner's departure, the cancer at the heart of this board has been excised. Right now, you've got a backlog of talented, honest doctors who need to be recommended to the state licensing board and credentialed to work in Akelton City. You also know of at least half a dozen doctors who bought their way through this board and have to be stopped before they do any further harm."

Doctor Welby dismissively waved his hand at the younger doctor. "Oh don't be ridiculous, Miles, we all know about your pet project on the west side. Many of those doctors you want to put out come from good families" He slammed his hand on the table, "and who cares if some negro has to wait an extra month or two before ...."

Griff interrupted. "Doctor Murdock believes that all of you were good men at one time! Perhaps some of you still are." He nodded at a uniformed officer who handed out folders to each member. "For those of you who

PRESCRIPTION FOR THE MOB

aren't, this is the information that we removed from a portable safe kept by Councilman Sinclair. Since none of it actually pertains to an open investigation, I'm under no legal requirement to keep it out of the hands of the press."

As the men shouted their displeasure, Griff interrupted again. "If any one of you doesn't play ball with the Doc here, all of you get exposed!"

"Ha!" One of the younger doctors, Killdare, laughed more. "I'll play along." He turned his folder upside down to show it contained nothing except blank paper. "You hypocrites voted me down every time I tried to do the right thing. I should let you all swing in the wind, but I still remember my Hippocratic Oath."

Miles Murdock grinned at that. "I was hoping you'd say that, Richard. That's why I want you to serve as the new head of the Recommendation Board. I'm certain you'll be voted in unanimously." As he looked around the room, each doctor raised his hand.

"Outstanding! Gentlemen, Captain Griffin and I will leave you now to get on with the business of Akelton City's health and welfare."

Killdare called out, "Try and stay off that ankle, Miles."

Miles Murdock looked down at the phony cast covering his right ankle and then back at his fellow physician, swinging his cane in Killdare's general direction. "That's the last time I go skiing this season." He limped out of the conference room smiling.

Captain Griffin threw one final comment at them. "Do what you want with those folders, gentlemen, just remember who has the original documents."

As both men stepped out in the morning sun, Griff stopped his friend. "How's the leg, Miles?"

"Dale did a great job sewing me up. She'd be a first class surgeon if I could convince her to go to medical school."

"Thanks for dropping off Edgerton yesterday."

"Thank Tommy and Dale. They were thrilled to get rid of the body." He looked at Dan's arm in the sling. "How's the shoulder?"

"It'll be fine in a few day" Griff hesitated for a moment. "Look, Miles, Hallick told me that several people have figured out I'm working with the Purple Scar. He hinted these same people are trying to figure out the Scar really is too."

"How far did he get?"

"I don't know yet. So far, nothing we've found in Hallick's apartment mentions you, but we haven't gone through everything yet. I'll be done in a day or so and then I'd like to talk to you, Dale and Tommy."

"Just let me know when."

That Friday, Dan met with everyone at the Swank Street Clinic. He had found nothing else to support Hallick's attempt to find out the Purple Scar's identity but felt everyone should know what the dying lieutenant had said to him.

"I was there when the team tore his place apart and we found nada. I don't think he was lying, though. There's no reason to hold back when the Grim Reaper's reaching for you."

"What about Parker or the rest of the conspirators?" Dale asked.

"We've found nothing there either. Some of these guys tuck stuff away in safety deposit boxes using false names or have another person hide it for them. That could be the case here."

The big cop shrugged. "I guess I'll be seeing less of you now, Miles." He looked at Dale again. "Get ready for a bigger phone bill."

"Maybe not, Griff. If there are people watching you and who you associate with; any sudden changes to your schedule or who you see or stop seeing would be viewed with suspicion."

Pedlar jumped in, "Then what do we do, Boss?"

"I'm going to have to be smarter about using the Purple Scar, Tommy. If there's a concerted effort to find out who is behind the mask then we have to obscure our trail as much as possible."

"It's time to go shopping then, Miles." Dale pointed at all three of them. "Before any of you crack wise about 'typical female', think about it. The Purple Scar has to be more than a mask now. New car, clothes, everything has to be exclusive to him and not linked to respected surgeon Miles Murdock."

"You've thought about this before now haven't you Dale?"

"Someone has to Dan. The three of you have been too busy the last two years getting shot at and beaten up to plan ahead." She turned her face to look at Miles. "I've accepted that you won't stop being the Purple Scar until you think Akelton City doesn't need him anymore, but it doesn't mean I have to like it and I won't stand by anymore and be quiet when I'm sewing up bullet wounds. You have to prepare for when it's time to burn the mask and that means staying alive long enough to see that day arrive."

Tommy chimed in. "This would be a great time to take Dale's advice, Doc. Friends of mine still in the business say that everyone is laying low right now. Bringing down Parker means the other bosses are dividing up his territory. They're sitting down in meeting halls and bosses' homes, trying to do it nice and quiet to avoid drawing attention from guys like you and Captain Griffin."

"Looks like it's already three votes in favor of laying low and shopping. Good thing we picked up some extra cash last week; right Tommy?"

Griff and Dale both responded. "What extra cash?"

"The Doc and I got into Parker's safe after the fireworks were over."

"I knew that safe was too empty when we opened it! You were going to tell me this when, Miles?" asked Griff.

The doctor smiled from ear to ear. "I'm telling you now, Griff; we came away with a little over $26,000. I was hoping we could figure out who Parker was squeezing the worst and get it back to them somehow. If there's anything left, we can always funnel that into Bill's clinic."

Dale pretended to pout, "There goes my new dress and vacation to Cuba."

The group laughed and began planning how to return the ill-gotten gains and keep the Purple Scar a man of mystery for awhile longer.

"This means no more looking over your shoulder, Bill. You should get used to being called Doctor Everett very soon." He put his hand out to the younger doctor. "Also, it's Miles from now on if that's okay with you."

The young physician looked up from the copy of the board's official recommendation to the older doctor and shook his hand. "Thank you, Miles." He looked down again and then back up. "Do I really want to know how you got that iceberg to go from a month's long wait to less than a week in making a decision?"

"The man who replaced Eldon Lochner as head of the board is an acquaintance of mine. With his help, I just appealed to their civic nature."

Doctor Everett looked hard at his fellow physician and then laughed. "That's a no then."

After a few more minutes discussing patients and the promise of dinner soon, Doctor Murdock left the clinic. He reflected as he walked that Dale was right about preparing for the future. Akelton City would need good doctors to go with policemen like Dan Griffin and politicians like Les Daniels. But until the time when that's all they needed, the Purple Scar would be there as well.

THE END

I THOUGHT THIS WAS A GOOD IDEA?

Whew! Here I thought the Domino Lady was considered obscure. Fortunately, a friend of mine has the reprint of Doctor Miles Murdock's original tales and lent it to me. Thanks Glen! It was daunting at first, but I finally figured out what the guys did from the first Airship 27 volume. Doc and his crew (sounds familiar for some reason) were almost a blank slate I could use to write a pulp love letter. Then I realized that means even more pressure to get it right and I suddenly felt like daunting my skull on the doorframe for taking this job.

In the first drafts, I had Maxie try to brace our hero in his free clinic, but it just didn't read right no matter how many times I rewrote it. A little research into charity work back in the 30s and 40s led me to problems in getting African-American doctors licensed at that time. This led to the creation of Doctor William Everett and then the first two pages made sense at last. Once I had that, the overall conspiracy started coming together and how the Purple Scar stumbled across it.

The armored auto came into play after I had about a third of the story written. I needed a good reason for Maxie to get caught in a lie and then killed by his boss after confessing everything. I also thought it would make a good macguffin to reveal the multiple double-crosses. Bad guys like Parker and Sinclair bumping each other off is a grand pulp tradition and I'm happy to continue it.

As much as I love the Age of Pulp though, one tradition I never understood was how easily the hero's support team gets smacked from behind, caught or were just incompetent. Yes, that also means I'm one of those guys who thinks a certain intrepid girl reporter got kidnapped way too often. So, I took advantage of the blank slate to give Tommy a new talent, advance Dale's medical skills and turn Griff into the kind of police officer that Akelton City needs to keep the other cops on the straight and narrow. Making Dale the voice of reason at the end also seemed like a natural thing for her.

Finally, I appreciate Ron for encouraging all of us write the macabre manhunter as a more vicious player in the war on crime and corruption. For a guy who suffered that kind of loss and then created his own, so very weird, alter-ego based on a dead brother; he should be closer to an unstoppable force than a cold and calculating vigilante. Threatening to cut pieces off a guy with a machete or setting him on fire should be as easy as breathing for a guy like the Purple Scar. Thanks again, Air Chief!

PAUL KEVIN FINDLEY - was raised by a kindly couple in a small town in Kansas. Unfortunately, he misplaced his blue suit and red cape as a child, so he has been a freelance writer for the last two years. This is his first published work in the wonderful, macabre world that is Pulp. For three years before that, he edited websites for a number of commercial businesses.

Prior to that, he served 20 years in the U.S. Air Force. He retired as a Logistics Specialist with the rank of Major back in 2009. During that time, he was able to travel and live in various places to include Austria, Japan, Egypt and many more. Surprisingly, he is still allowed in all of those countries. He is married with two kids still at home and more scattered throughout the U.S.

His wife is very happy he finally listened to her and took up writing as something other than a hobby. It keeps him home, makes a few bucks and keeps him out of trouble for the most part. If you want to tell him how much you loved his tale of the Purple Scar or even if you didn't you can contact him at www.linkedin.com/pub/kevin-findley/35/208/36a/. Expect more from him at Airship 27 and other Pulp-related corners of the internet.

TRIAL BY FIRE

BY ERIK FRANKLIN

Dr. Phillip Caldwell removed his spectacles and wearily massaged the bridge of his nose. He had been laboring on his speech all night, and it *still* needed a great deal of revising. Setting down his pen on the notepad, Caldwell rose from the desk and began to pace around his apartment, as if some form of inspiration would be hiding among the sleek, polished furniture. The luxury apartment that he lived in was spacious, and it loomed even larger with the absence of his wife. Mrs. Caldwell was visiting her family in London, and he wished to be by her side, but he had made a previous commitment to give a lecture at Akelton University.

As Caldwell strolled around the room, he kept wishing that his wife were with him. Truth be told, she was the brilliant one, giving his speeches the dynamic flair that had made him a popular lecturer. He had received an angry phone call earlier that day from one of his patients, the very one on whom his lecture was to be based. The patient insisted that Caldwell never mention his name, or his case, to anyone. He had previously consented, so this abrupt change was most alarming to Caldwell.

This unexpected setback left Caldwell in a difficult position. He had hoped that by using this man as an example, he would be able to generate more interest in his theory and gain more support within the psychological community. Caldwell looked to the phone on his desk, and decided to call his patient back. He could easily understand why the man would be resistant to the idea of being the focus of the lecture. After all, who wants to expose one's darkest thoughts to the world? However, if Caldwell could explain the situation to him, if he could persuade him that he would be making a tremendous contribution to psychology, then perhaps the man would listen to reason.

He dialed the patient's phone number, but received no answer. Perhaps he was busy, but Caldwell doubted this. According to their sessions, the patient went to bed early and rarely went out in the evenings. He probably ignored the phone, to the doctor's chagrin. Caldwell went back to his notes and read through them once again, hoping to find another angle for his speech. No matter what approach he attempted, it was no use... Caldwell *had* to use this patient for his lecture if he was to prove his point. He was the perfect case! Putting on his hat and coat, Caldwell decided to drive to the man's home and meet with him face to face.

Caldwell locked his apartment door behind him and began walking down the hall. The doctor paused for a moment as a strange sound caught his attention. It sounded like a woman's scream, followed by an intense howling of wind. Soon the woman's scream was joined by more cries of terror from the people on the floor beneath him. Then an unusual sensation began to fill the air: intense heat. The temperature of the floor began to rise rapidly, and the smell of burning wood reached Dr. Caldwell's nose. The building was on fire!

Assuming that the floor beneath him would be impassable, he thought of the fire escape outside his window. Fumbling with his key, Caldwell hastily jammed it into the lock and pushed against the door. His attention was diverted by the same sound of howling wind, only this time it was much closer. Looking towards the staircase at the end of the hall, he saw a jet of flames, like the breath of a dragon, scorching the walls. Curiously, the stream of fire stopped abruptly, and the sound of heavy footsteps could be heard over the crackling fire.

Not wasting any more time, Caldwell gave his key a final twist which unlocked the door. He raced to the fire escape window and started to unfasten it. As he worked feverishly, the doctor could hear the heavy footsteps growing closer and closer, accompanied by howling jets of fire. A horrifying thought occurred to Caldwell... was this person after him?

Putting a leg outside the window and onto the fire escape, Caldwell looked back into his apartment, and his jaw dropped. The whole place was an inferno; streams of fire were blasting from a shadowy figure in the hall. Though the intense heat distorted his vision, Caldwell saw a hulking figure standing among the flames. The fire cast an orange glow on him, revealing that the figure was wearing a thick, iron plated metal suit. The flames concealed the brutish figure's face. He was holding something in his hands. It resembled a fire hose, but it was too dark and metallic. The man inspected his handiwork from the hallway, and shot another stream of flames from his apparatus towards Caldwell!

The doctor ducked, but not before he felt the searing hand of the flames strike his face. He felt his flesh burn as he frantically attempted to stifle the fire spreading across his suit! Caldwell descended the fire escape rapidly and ran out into the street. He jointed the other survivors who had gathered to watch their former homes burn, and he was horrified to see that there were only a few people around him. Gathering his thoughts,

Caldwell realized, with great shock, that he might be among a handful of people that saw The Blaze and survived.

Previous headlines raced through the doctor's mind. It all began a few weeks ago. Akelton City had been caught in a grip of terror by an arsonist whom the newspapers had dubbed "The Blaze". Thirteen buildings had burned to the ground with few survivors and no witnesses. There was no explanation and no end in sight.

Seeing that he was burned, a few medical workers grabbed him and placed Caldwell in an ambulance. Caldwell began to feel faint as he saw the doors close and drifted into unconsciousness. The doctor was tormented by feverish nightmares about a man in the metal suit, surrounded by fire, stalking him.

Elsewhere in Akelton City, another man was suffering through a different nightmare. Moments before, James Roscoe had considered himself to be untouchable. One of the most notorious crime bosses in Akelton City, he moved in the highest social circles with impunity. The police had been at him for years, but he was too clever for them. Roscoe had stepped outside of his favorite restaurant to enjoy a Cuban cigar. As he removed the cigar, a folded note fell out of his pocket. It was a threatening letter reminding him of a bribe that he had yet to pay. Roscoe laughed as he tossed it in the garbage. It would be cheaper to pay his enforcers to deal with it than to give in to the note's demands. Roscoe was about to join his party back in the restaurant when he was suddenly seized by the collar and yanked into a dark alleyway. A chloroformed rag was thrust in his face and Roscoe felt his body succumb.

When Roscoe awoke, he was hanging upside down, watching the lights of the city as he swayed back and forth. He recognized the area as the construction site of one of the apartments he had ordered built, except that he had never seen it from the top floor of the steel construction beams. Roscoe had made the mistake of looking down, where he saw the six story plunge he would take if his captor decided to let go. He felt strong hands holding his ankles in a vice-like grip. Roscoe tried to get a look at his captor, but his face was too dark to see, obscured by the shadows of a fedora.

"Now tell me the truth..." his captor demanded of him. His voice was raspy, menacing, and it chilled the crime boss to the bone. "...you ordered those buildings burned to the ground."

"What?" Roscoe squeaked pathetically, having no idea what the man was referring to.

"The Blaze! You hired him to destroy your buildings so you could collect on the insurance! Confess or die!"

At this point, the captor lowered Roscoe dramatically, giving the crime lord a sample of the fate that was his destiny if he did not confess. Roscoe screamed and pleaded.

"I'm telling you, I had nothing to do with it! You *have* to believe me!"

"I don't have to do anything!" his captor shouted back.

Roscoe felt a mighty pull on his legs, as he was lifted and placed roughly on the steel beam. No longer at the mercy of gravity, he hugged the large piece of metal as tears of relief streamed down his face. Roscoe was premature in his celebration. Seconds later he felt his captor's hand grab his shoulder and flip him on his back.

"Look at me when I'm talking to you!"

Roscoe stared into the most horrific face that he had ever seen. He wanted to scream, but the sound could not escape his throat. Roscoe's hands twitched in terror and he began to sputter incoherently. The grotesque countenance of the man paralyzed his reasoning ability. The corpse-like face was dark and sickly purple in color. It had the black, sunken eyes of a skull, and its face was covered with acid burns and hideous scars.

"You're... you're..." Roscoe said, terrified to speak the man's name.

"Yes. I am the Purple Scar!" the vigilante declared to the crime boss. He picked the man up by his collar with ease and held him aloft. Roscoe wanted desperately to look away, his heart was pounding with fear, but for some inexplicable reason, he could not. He was completely overcome by the Purple Scar's dark, soulless eyes.

"Tell me the truth or die!" the Purple Scar demanded once more in his raspy, unearthly growl.

"Now... now listen to me... this is the God's honest truth!" Roscoe began, attempting to get a hold of himself. "I had nothing to do with this! These fires... I don't know anything about them! I swear! I swear on my mother's grave!"

"You owned six of the buildings that were torched. The insurance money would have made you a pretty penny! You've done this before and I can prove it!"

"Purple Scar... I'm already a wealthy man... and... and... what about the other buildings that weren't mine? What reason would I have to torch them? Yes, okay... I burned down my dock warehouse, I admit it... but that was different!"

"How? How is it different? You are merely hiding your buildings with the rest. A needle in the haystack to confuse the police!" The Purple Scar said as he tightened his grip on the man. Roscoe began to shake once again.

"No! No! You've got to believe me! If I were going to set a fire, I'd make it seem like an accident, and I sure as hell wouldn't have killed all those people! That raises too many questions! I burned down the docks at night when nobody was there!"

After a few moments of thought, the Purple Scar set Roscoe down once again. He was a master in the art of psychology, and after weighing Roscoe's frightened responses and revealing body language; the Purple Scar reluctantly came to the conclusion that this was not his man. James Roscoe had not become the man he was through excessive force and violence. He was known as a manipulator, and preferred discreet methods.

The Purple Scar grumbled to himself. James Roscoe was the only connection that he could find with the fires, and now his theory proved to be useless. He would have to approach this case from a different angle, perhaps there was something he overlooked in his research. As the sworn protector of Akelton City, the Purple Scar had made The Blaze his number one enemy, but he had no idea of how to find him.

"Can... can I leave?" Roscoe asked sheepishly, his body still shaking.

The Purple Scar turned to glare at Roscoe for interrupting his thoughts. Though he failed to capture The Blaze, the Purple Scar was determined that the night would not be a total loss. Removing something from his black overcoat, the Purple Scar once again thrust the chloroform rag onto the crime boss' face.

When the dapper crime boss awoke, he was tied to a lamppost outside of police headquarters. Captain Dan Griffin walked outside, cutting through the curious crowd of onlookers and reporters. His large, robust arms reached around and untied Roscoe from the lamppost. Griffin's normally rock hard face wore a small, unexpected smile this day.

"Thank you, officer." Roscoe said distractedly as he stepped away from the lamppost, but Griffin put a large hand on his shoulder.

"Where do you think you're going, Mr. Roscoe?"

"Why... to my club..." he said hesitatingly.

"I don't think so..." said Griffin, the smile broadening on his square jaw "...you are coming with me."

"What? Why? What's the charge?" Roscoe said, starting to regain the smooth, slick composure that he was accustomed to presenting the police.

"Insurance fraud and arson for starters." Griffin said as he fastened handcuffs around Roscoe's wrists.

"I have no idea what you are talking about!" Roscoe protested. Then he thought back to his interrogation with the Purple Scar. He had confessed to those crimes in his presence, but they were on top of a building under construction... there was no way that anyone could have overheard them!

Griffin reached into Roscoe's inner jacket pocket and removed a slip of crumpled up paper. The police captain inspected it with a knowing smile. Roscoe felt the blood drain from his face as a feeling of dread swept over him. He knew exactly what the note was.

"To Mr. Roscoe, if you do not pay us as promised, we will go to the police and tell them that you ordered us to be silent while your men burned down the docks. We ask that each man be fairly compensated for the loss of his job – The Dock Workers." Griffin read this aloud, enjoying watching the reporters frantically scribbling down every word with industrious zeal.

The Purple Scar claimed that he had the evidence to convict Roscoe, and when he grabbed him by the collar, he must have slipped the note into his coat pocket! The Purple Scar must have picked it up from the alley! There was no way Roscoe could worm his way out of this trap. Griffin began to whistle an upbeat tune as reporters rounded on Roscoe with questions about his arrest.

The Purple Scar entered his private quarters with a sigh. Although he spent his time amongst the worst elements of society, the vigilante had all the comforts that a mansion on Swank Street would provide. He peeled the mask from his face and enjoyed the feeling of air on his skin. Underneath the hideous mask of the Purple Scar was the handsome, chiseled face of Miles Murdock, M.D. Though Murdock spent his nights terrorizing criminals, his days were dedicated to healing patients at the operating theater in his mansion, or at the free clinic he maintained on Down Street. He vowed to help the people of Akelton City in any way that he could.

Running his hand through his curly black hair, he placed his Purple Scar mask inside the wall safe. His study reflected the tastes of a world traveler. The room was richly furnished with antiques from the four corners of the globe, and the paneled walls were decorated with his collection of death masks. Ever since the brutal murder of his brother, Miles Murdock had become obsessed with symbols of death and hunting artifacts. The Purple Scar mask that Murdock had sculpted was a grotesque tribute to his dead brother. His brother's face had been savagely ravaged and disfigured by criminals who had cruelly poured acid on it for their sadistic pleasure. Murdock, though repulsed by the sight of his brother's mangled face, had used its image as an inspiration for his crusade to bring justice to Akelton City. He had studied plastic surgery and psychology at the university, and trained himself in the fighting arts of jiu-jitsu and savate to become the Purple Scar. To prepare himself for his fight with the underworld, Murdock had conducted extensive research in criminology. The mask of the Purple Scar was meant to inflict the same fear upon the underworld that they brought to innocent people of Akelton City.

Though Murdock did not require much sleep to keep going, he sunk himself deep into a leather chair by the fire to relax. Murdock cast his eyes upon a collection of African hunting spears that were mounted on the wall above the mantle. He had put the notorious James Roscoe behind bars, but his main target, The Blaze, was still at large. He found it appropriate that his thoughts would drift to hunting in a room he dedicated to that very thing.

He had hoped that a few hours of rest would have rejuvenated his spirit and given him a fresh perspective on his hunt for The Blaze, but alas, Murdock was unable to find a new angle when he awoke. Checking his itinerary, Murdock saw that the rest of the day was relatively free. He breathed a sigh of relief, knowing that he could fully dedicate his mind to the capture of The Blaze.

After a quick shower and breakfast, Murdock went back to the hunt... at least from his study. Spreading out the various newspaper clippings that he had saved on his desk, Murdock poured over the articles. Juicy, sensational journalism was accompanied by dramatic photographs of the fires. His eyes skimmed through the text, hoping to find another link, but other than the fact that they were the work of The Blaze, there was nothing to be found. He had marked the locations of the fires on a map of Akelton City, but they were too far apart to indicate a pattern of any kind.

When Murdock found himself unable to think clearly, he decided to continue working on a sculpture that he started earlier in the week. When he struggled with a case, Murdock often resorted to his favorite hobby of sculpting. He was grateful that he had not begun the fine detail work on this one, for he was looking forward to digging deep and working the clay with his hands. When Murdock finished, it would be a perfect replica of a rhinoceros ready to charge... at least he hoped so.

Murdock turned on the radio, needing the ambient noise to keep him company. This broadcast happened to be about college football, specifically about his Alma Matter, Akleton University. He allowed his thoughts to drift back to the football field at the university, and then idly thought of the letters he earned in his other sports: boating, riflery, and swimming. Sighing, Murdock often found himself wishing to return to that simpler time.

Putting on an apron, Murdock kneaded the clay, forcing it into the desired shape. He worked out his mounting tension with each piece. Privately, he was frustrated that the organized crime angle had amounted to nothing. This meant that The Blaze was a lone operative with his own agenda. The case would require far more work than he had anticipated. During his extensive self-study of the criminal mind, he had, of course, read about arsonists. As he was mentally going through what he knew about arsonists, a knock at the door caught him off guard.

Racing to answer it, he realized that his appointment with Dale Jordan had completely slipped his mind. He hastily wiped the clay from his hands on his apron as he turned the knob. He was met by one of the loveliest women in Akelton City. Dale, his assistant and chief nurse, was blessed with an attractive oval face, framed with auburn hair. She smiled as she looked at the clay smeared on his apron.

"I can see you're hard at work," she said with a slight giggle.

"Yes, I've been trying to clear my head," he admitted, as he motioned her inside. He closed the door behind her.

"Well, I'm anxious to see it," Dale said as she accompanied him to his study. "You know I always love looking at your sculptures."

"It's... not as far along as I'd like it to be." Murdock admitted.

Before he could show her his progress on the rhinoceros, Dale's attention was diverted by the multitude of Blaze newspaper clippings strewn across his desk. Murdock silently cursed to himself, annoyed that he had forgotten to hide the articles from her prying eyes. There were only a handful of people that knew of his double life as the Purple Scar, and Dale was one of them. Though Murdock knew that she would never divulge his secret, he wanted to keep her away from the dangerous life that he chose to lead. She skimmed through the articles and turned to Murdock with interest.

"So, no luck on finding this Blaze character?" she asked.

"No. I thought I had a lead on him, but no dice." he said bitterly. "Dale, would you like to look at the sculpture?" Murdock ventured, trying to prevent her from getting involved. He might as well have tried to stop a moving train with his bare hands.

"In a minute," she murmured "...this is fascinating," Dale said as she looked the photographs and then at the map Murdock had created. "So what lead didn't pan out?"

"Organized crime. They're not paying The Blaze to burn down buildings. He must be acting on his own."

"And you haven't found anything to link them?"

"No," Murdock said bitterly. He strolled over to the articles and watched as Dale focused her emerald green eyes on each picture. Suddenly, her eyes lit up, and she turned to Murdock.

"Miles, I know that this may sound crazy, but I think I've found something," she said cautiously, though the excitement in her voice was evident.

Murdock flew to her side with great surprise. "You did? Where? How?"

She shot him a defiant look. "Now you shouldn't be too surprised, Miles. I'm pretty clever myself."

"I didn't mean it like that." he said, irritated. He desperately wanted to hear Dale's thoughts, and this idle conversation was maddening to him.

"You know I could be a real asset to you." she said with a knowing expression. Even though Dale understood Murdock's reasoning, she could not help but feel frustrated that there were parts of his life that he kept secret from her. One day, perhaps, he might break down, and she would be there for him.

"You already are," said Murdock sincerely. "Now what have you found?"

She turned back to the photographs and pulled a few articles from the spread. She rearranged them in front of Murdock and pointed at the first one.

"Look, this man is in all of these pictures." Dale said definitively as she checked each photograph again. Murdock squinted as he bent down to look at the man she was pointing at. The photographer was more interested in the fire than the crowd, so his face was out of focus. Nevertheless, he could see a small man standing in the crowd, who could not have been more than five foot four, looking at the fire. The man was wearing a respectable, if unremarkable suit, had a severe crew cut, and the lenses of his circular glasses appeared a solid white reflection in the photograph. Due to the camera's focus, it was impossible to determine the man's expression or emotional state.

Seeing that Murdock had finished examining the photograph, Dale laid the second photograph over the first. An apartment on Down Street was ablaze and firemen were rushing to and fro to quell the raging inferno. It was a dramatic photograph, but Dale pointed to the crowd once more. In between some other onlookers, one could barely discern a small man hidden amongst them. The same crew cut and a similar looking suit.

"But that might not be him," Murdock said, playing devil's advocate. Undeterred, Dale placed a third photograph in front of him.

A similar fire, but this time the man's profile could be seen with complete clarity because he was standing next to the cameraman. Murdock looked up at Dale, beginning to believe the connection. Dale quickly showed him where the man stood in the next few photographs. Although some of the photos were questionable, it was clear in Murdock's mind that this man was at several of the fires.

"Perhaps he lives around there?" Murdock said. He had already followed one lead to a dead end, and did not wish to be involved in another wild goose chase.

Thinking quickly, Dale grabbed the map and indicated the locations of the fires with the corresponding photographs.

"Either he's got the most convoluted commute of all time, or he has extraordinarily bad luck," Dale said "these places are too far apart and unconnected for any single person to get to..."

"Unless he knows something about the fires..." Murdock said, coming around to Dale's way of thinking. "Thank you, Dale. I've been studying the articles and photos for hours and hours, and you waltz in and give me a new lead before you take off your coat!"

She shrugged with a smile "It's like you say when examining your patients, examine everything and don't twist the facts to fit a theory."

"Yes," he said with a grimace, knowing that he had made the same mistake earlier when he went after Roscoe.

"In any case, I'm glad that the Purple Scar put Roscoe behind bars. It's high time that that crook got what was coming to him!" she said, sensing Murdock's thoughts and trying to comfort him. In the operating room she was able to anticipate his every move and request, and Murdock realized that her abilities overlapped in his personal life.

Suddenly, the sports announcer of the football game was interrupted by an urgent newsflash. Murdock had completely forgotten about the

"Look, this man is in all the pictures."

radio during his talk with Dale, but now that the monotone was broken, he was paying strict attention.

"We interrupt this broadcast to bring you the following message!" a man said in hurried tones. "Another fire has broken out, this time at the Foster Boarding House! The fire department is on its way and the police have cordoned off the area. We suspect that once again this is the work of The Blaze! We will provide you with further updates as they happen..."

Murdock sprang into action. He equipped himself with the Purple Scar's standard gear: his special coat (it contained a secret pocket where he kept the Purple Scar's mask), hat, a set of master keys, pencil flashlight, police badge, .38 revolver, and his specialized fountain pen that could eject a stream of black fluid when needed. Murdock turned to Dale while he prepared himself.

"Dale, stay here and if anybody calls, tell them I'm out."

"Where should I say you are?" she asked.

"Tell them I'm caught in traffic. If I get to the fire in time, I may catch your mystery man!"

+++

Miles Murdock's black sedan raced through the streets of Akelton City. He was familiar with the Foster Boarding House; it was not too far from his clinic on Down Street. It would make sense for him to be seen in the area, so he could move about without attracting attention. Murdock thought of the diminutive man that Dale had discovered in the news clippings. True, he did not look like an arsonist or a murderer; he appeared to be the sort of man that is easy to overlook. Still, that may have been his strength, moving about unnoticed with murder in his heart. Even though he discounted it earlier, Murdock thought of the one thread that tied these cases together: every building that was burned was an apartment building, boardinghouse, or home of some kind. This man, if he was indeed the Purple Scar's target, was specifically looking to burn people alive!

Looking ahead, Murdock saw a traffic jam further up the road with smoke rising in the distance. He was in the right place. Parking his car on the side of the road, Murdock got out of his black sedan and ran towards the fire. If he was able to find the man in the crowd, Murdock made up his mind to tail him. It was rare for the Purple Scar to emerge in the daytime, his disguise being its most frightening at night, but he had to risk it. Perhaps if he could grab the man and lure him into a darkened alley, Murdock would be able to achieve the similar horrifying effect for the Purple Scar. Murdock wondered how a man would react to the mask, for few people could look upon the Scar's countenance and maintain their nerve.

Reaching the crowd, Murdock made a feigned interest in observing the fire. To his relief, he saw that the fire department had the flames under control, but his heart was heavy when he saw several bodies being carried out on stretchers... the blankets covering their faces.

Damn him! Murdock thought to himself.

Feeling that he had played the part of curious onlooker long enough, he began to scan the crowd. One thing that Murdock had learned in hunting down criminals was to start his search by looking for their height. His eyes lowered to approximate the man's size and after a few moments of combing the crowd, he found the man nestled among the crowd of people. The fire was reflected in his large, circular spectacles, and Murdock could swear he saw a look of awe on the man's face. His mouth was agape, his brown eyes mesmerized by the fire. The man looked as if he were watching the most beautiful light show in the world unfolding before his eyes.

Murdock felt his fist tighten and restrained himself. He had a plan, and he would stick to it. Time passed slowly as the firemen heroically battled with the flames. Eventually their orange glow faded and the flames stopped flickering, leaving a billowing cloud of thick grey smoke in their absence. As soon as the flames died down, so did the man's interest. He discreetly left the crowd and began to walk away in an unassuming manner. Murdock too left his position and quietly pushed through the onlookers.

The man strolled to the intersection and checked carefully before walking across the street. Murdock spied a dark alley nearby and decided that now he would make his move. Everyone else in the area was preoccupied with the fire, so they would not notice the abduction of a seemingly harmless little man.

The meek, little man was whistling to himself. *A singularly odd reaction to having seen dead, charred bodies at a fire,* Murdock thought to himself as he quickened his pace, starting to catch up with the man. *He is making a bold act of casualness, as if trying to prove to the world that despite his small stature, he is made of sterner stuff.*

Slipping the revolver out of his pocket, he stealthily pressed it against the man's back. He heard the man make a small yelp, like that of a frightened dog. His hands flew up, but Murdock barked at him in hushed tones.

"Put your hands down!"

The man obeyed as he looked around for help, but another press from Murdock's gun made him keep walking. He tried to get a look at Murdock, but was growled at again.

"Head into that alleyway if you value your life."

"I... I don't have any money." the man said. He spoke quickly, his voice high pitched and squeaky.

"Just go in!" Murdock said through gritted teeth. He was careful not to use his natural voice, so the man would not be able to identify him as Miles Murdock or the Purple Scar. As they passed by a drug store window, Murdock tipped his hat. He caught the man looking at the window, trying to catch the reflection of his kidnapper, but the hat blocked his face.

"Over there, by the trashcans."

The man obeyed, stopping in front of the filthy metal receptacles. Murdock needed time to slip the mask on, and considering that the man kept trying to see his face, he had to incapacitate him without serious injury. So Murdock shoved the man into the trashcans. The man crumpled to the dirty concrete floor with a gasp of pain, using his arm to brace himself against the grimy brick wall. Taking the opportunity, Murdock reached into the secret pocket of his special coat and removed the face of the Purple Scar.

Getting up, the man turned around, but he was not prepared for the full on effect of the Purple Scar's mask. His brown eyes bulged with fear as the small man shrank even further. The Purple Scar towered over him and pointed his .38 snub nose revolver into the man's face.

"You're... you're the Purple Scar!" he said, tears forming in his eyes as his mouth trembled.

"I know," the dark vigilante said, "and who are you?"

"I'm... my name is Alvin Shams! I'm nobody! What do you want with me? I haven't done anything wrong!"

The Purple Scar was watching Alvin's eyes and body language closely, studying for any telltale signs of lying or deception. So far, he saw none, but this was just the beginning of his interrogation.

"You were watching the fire, Alvin." the Purple Scar said in his raspy voice, ending the sentence with a menacing note.

"Yes, yes I was! There were dozens of people there!" Alvin protested as he pressed himself against the wall.

"You were also at the Jones Street fire, the Parkington Hotel fire, the..." the Purple Scar began to recite the list of locations that Dale had pulled from the newspaper clippings. On a whim, the Purple Scar decided to throw in a few of the locations that Dale was not able to spot Alvin at. "— the 3rd Avenue Apartment fire—"

"What? How can you...you can't prove that!" Alvin snapped, his face turning white with fear. The Purple Scar was beginning to sense a reaction in him. He did not display any of the classic signs of lying: aversion of the eyes, hesitation of speech, over rehearsed answers, yet why did the names of those locations cause him such distress?

"I never trust a man who tells me to "prove it"!" The Purple Scar shot back, causing Alvin to squirm. "Furthermore, there are photos placing you at the majority of the fires. I suggest you read the Akelton Gazette more carefully."

"So what if I was at those fires? Akelton is a small city! I'm sure a lot of people saw more than one of the fires!" Alvin said, anger starting to replace his fear. According to most psychological studies, the angrier a man got during an interrogation, the more likely he was telling the truth. Still, the Purple Scar had his doubts.

"The city is not that small. Perhaps maybe one or two fires could be witnessed, but Alvin... you were seen at *all* of them! You set each of the fires, Alvin Shams!" he said, leaning in close to Alvin's sweaty face. The small man turned his head, doing his best not to see the hideous, corpse-like mask of the Purple Scar.

"I did not! I did not! I did not! It was not me! I did not do it! You have to believe me!" Alvin said defiantly.

"Why does everyone keep saying that I *have* to believe them!" the Purple Scar spat out in frustration. By now, he had made a thorough examination of Alvin Shams' mental state under duress, and concluded that while the man was not overtly lying... he had some connection, however tenuous, to these fires. Alvin Shams did not match the physical description of The Blaze by any stretch of the imagination. Perhaps he was working with a large, hulking accomplice.

It was time to lure him, or them, into a trap. Alvin Shams did not strike one as an intelligent man, and if the Purple Scar left the right bait...

"Very well, Alvin, I'll leave you be for now, but I will be watching you!" the Purple Scar said threateningly. He started to walk away. "I have some leads to follow up on at the Roscoe dockside warehouse. You don't happen to work at the docks, do you Alvin?"

"No, I'm a draftsman for the Grand Continental Railway," he pleaded.

"Then you should have nothing to fear tonight, Alvin."

The Purple Scar wandered back into the street, leaving Alvin shaking in his shoes. There was something about Alvin, something that bothered him. If Alvin took the bait, he would most likely contact whoever he knew (possibly The Blaze himself, the Purple Scar hoped) and send him to dispatch the Purple Scar at the Roscoe docks that night. Anticipating a possible showdown, the Purple Scar thought of one place that he knew would be vacant: the abandoned, burned out remains of Roscoe's insurance fraud. If The Blaze did show himself, at least he would be near water should things get out of hand. The Purple Scar debated calling the police, but ultimately decided against it. The Blaze was a terrible new opponent, and he did not want to risk Captain Griffin or his men's lives in the battle. The Purple Scar hoped that he would be able to stop The Blaze this night.

It will be a trial by fire, the Purple Scar thought to himself.

The Purple Scar became Miles Murdock once again and continued on with his day, though much of it was a blur to him. His mind kept wandering back to Alvin Shams and the trap that he had set. As the day wound to a close, Murdock bid Dale a good night, and then opened the safe to remove his mask.

Once more the Purple Scar went out into the night, hoping to find and vanquish The Blaze. However, the Purple Scar kept wondering if he had made a huge mistake. What if Alvin were innocent and had no connection to The Blaze? What if, while the Purple Scar was wasting his time at the Akelton docks, The Blaze was elsewhere murdering more innocent people? He tried his best to put these thoughts out of his head as he arrived at the docks.

Parking his black sedan some distance away, the Purple Scar crept around the burned out docks like a demon lurking in the shadows. He could neither see nor hear anyone, and this filled him with relief. If The Blaze did show up, at least the two could face each other alone with no chance of any bystanders getting hurt.

Examining the burned wreckage of the dock warehouses, the Purple Scar thought back to Roscoe's story of the arson. Roscoe had really done a number on this place. Perhaps he was a little overzealous in the destruction of his own property. Walking among the blackened pieces of wood and debris, he decided that he would put his mind at ease with a phone call to Captain Dan Griffin. He still did not want him or the police to be involved, but he needed to know everything he could about Alvin Shams. Perhaps he had underworld connections or a history of arson? There was only one way to find out.

There was a payphone across the street from the charred buildings. Seeing that the area was devoid of human life, the Purple Scar figured that he could call without being seen. The phone booth also concealed his shape in the shadows, allowing him to keep surveillance on the docks in case The Blaze was to appear.

He dialed Griffin's private number and waited to be connected.

"Hello, this is Captain Griffin," Griffin said over the phone. His voice sounded tired from the long hours he was putting in.

"Captain, I need you to do something for me..." the Purple Scar said into the phone.

The Purple Scar heard an audible shudder come from Griffin over the phone.

"Damn you, Scar, you scared the Dickens out of me!" Griffin said, regaining his composure. "Why don't you talk in your normal voice over the phone? We both know who you are."

It was true. Captain Griffin was one of a select few that knew of Miles Murdock's double life as the Purple Scar. The two had often worked together, unofficially of course, to deal with the crime in Akelton City. Griffin had a habit of "letting things slip" in Murdock's presence, and the Purple Scar always informed Griffin of any evidence he was able to uncover. Griffin had built up a tolerance to the grotesque face of the Purple Scar, but he always found the cold, raspy, whisper-like voice chilling.

"Eavesdroppers," the Purple Scar said by way of an explanation, much to the dismay of Griffin. He would be forced to listen to that dreaded voice for the duration of the conversation. "Now here is what I need from you... I need you to investigate a certain individual."

"Who is he?" Griffin said, and the Purple Scar could hear the Captain rustling some papers on his desk and grabbing a pen.

"Alvin Shams."

"Alvin... Shams..." repeated Griffin as he wrote the name down. "What's he supposed to have done?"

"He may be involved with The Blaze."

"The Blaze!" Griffin yelled. "It's about time somebody's come up with a lead on that maniac! What's the connection?"

"I'm not sure..." the Purple Scar admitted "He's been in the crowd at every fire since The Blaze began his attacks."

"How do you know that?"

"I interrogated him earlier today... he was not lying to me, but Alvin Shams definitely has something to hide."

"One look at your face and he didn't confess to everything, huh?" Griffin said, mildly amused. "I guess that there's a first time for everything."

"I can't prove anything at the moment... but there is something about him I don't trust."

"What?"

"I'm not sure."

"You're not giving me much to go on here..." Griffin said, starting to feel frustrated.

"I'm sorry, but I know he has something to do with The Blaze." The Purple Scar insisted.

"I'll check into him, but this sounds tenuous at best. If I find anything, I'll give you a call and we can discuss this." Griffin said with little optimism in his voice, thinking of the Purple Scar's earlier failure. True, he was delighted to have Roscoe behind bars, but The Blaze was a much greater and more sensational threat.

"The psychology points to him, Captain. Alvin Shams fits the mental profile of an arsonist." The Purple Scar continued, feeling that he had to defend his theory to Griffin. "Arsonists often return to the scene of their crimes. They find watching the flames to be... pleasurable. The look I saw on Alvin's face while he was looking at the burning building was one of pure, sadistic joy."

"I'll look into it... is there anything else that the police can do for you?" he said, a subtle mocking tone in his voice.

"Hang on... I may have just caught someone in my trap!" The Purple Scar said. He had been watching the building the entire time. Out of the corner of his eye, The Purple Scar had noticed a large figure lurching towards the burned out building. He had never laid eyes on The Blaze before, but the shape matched the descriptions that eyewitnesses had been giving the newspapers.

Pulling out his .38 snub nose revolver, the Purple Scar circled around to the other entrance of the building in order to get a better look at the man. After the fire, the whole area had remained abandoned, and this structure, a former warehouse still filled to the brim with boxes of burned goods, offered plenty of cover should bullets start flying.

The Purple Scar did not want to risk making another mistake and decided that he had better be sure of his target. Crouching in the shadows behind some boxes, the Purple Scar waited as he heard heavy, metallic footsteps drawing near. The Purple Scar called out:

"Blaze!" His ghoulish voice echoed through the large, abandoned building. The Purple Scar heard metal shifting against metal as he rose to get a detailed look at the arsonist.

Though he was no stranger to unusual criminals and their depraved minds, he could not help but be taken aback by what he saw. The Blaze was covered from head-to-toe in a plated, iron suit. The armor was crude, as if forged and hammered by hand. The metal itself was blackened and tarnished by the many fires he had waded through. His arms and legs were unusually long, giving him gorilla-like proportions. He wore a welder's mask, but had welded it onto bands of metal in order to fashion himself a makeshift helmet. The Blaze was much larger than the Purple Scar, and the vigilante knew that a physical confrontation would only end in his demise.

The Blaze carried a strange object clasped in his hands. It was a thick tube with a head like a fire hose, connected to a large canister that was mounted on his back. A hissing sound came from the device and The Blaze had his finger resting against a trigger. The Purple Scar did not remember seeing a weapon like this before, but instinctively knew that it was to be feared. The Purple Scar deduced that The Blaze had built his own metal, fireproof suit, and was careful to leave the carnage before the heat got too severe and melted his armor.

The Purple Scar held his comparatively small snub nose .38 revolver tightly in his hand as The Blaze stared at him, shifting his weapon over to target the vigilante. They were studying each other for weaknesses, and the Purple Scar had a sinking feeling that The Blaze was having more luck than he was.

"Blaze, stop what you are doing!" the Purple Scar yelled, but he had a feeling that his words would fall on deaf ears.

"No! You can't stop me!" The Blaze yelled back. Other than the voice sounding deep and savage, the Purple Scar could gather nothing else from his speech. He was speaking through a metal mask, which made the task of understanding him even more difficult.

"You know too much, Purple Scar! Burn in hell!" The Blaze yelled as he pulled the trigger on his weapon. The Purple Scar's eyes widened as he leapt from the titanic stream of fire that belched forth from the hideous

"Blaze!"

flame thrower. Hiding behind another stack of boxes, the Purple Scar watched as the area where he stood moments before was immolated by The Blaze.

Sticking his head up, the Purple Scar watched as The Blaze shot another stream of fire towards him. The Purple Scar raced between piles of boxes, avoiding The Blaze's jets of flames as he sought some kind of vantage point. Although The Blaze's armor made him fireproof, it also slowed him down. The Purple Scar was able to circle to the side of the metal man and he began firing with his pistol before The Blaze could shift his position.

The Purple Scar's shots, though on target, ricocheted harmlessly off The Blaze's iron armor. As bullets bounced randomly off of The Blaze, they collided with the boxes surrounding him. Shooting him was proving more of a risk than a legitimate strategy, so the Purple Scar pocketed his pistol as he hastily struggled to come up with a new plan. Crouching behind a stack of wooden crates, the Purple Scar went through his various gadgets, but he failed to see how any of them could be useful in this situation. His ears pricked up as he heard the distinctive footfalls of The Blaze growing closer, and the Purple Scar wheeled around just in time to see a box falling on top of him!

While the Purple Scar was hiding behind them, The Blaze had rammed the stack of crates with a shoulder rush. The Purple Scar sprang out of the way, but since he did not have time to properly prepare his jump, his leap fell short and his right leg was pinned by the uppermost wooden crate. The wood of the crate was burned and weakened, mercifully reducing the weight placed on the Purple Scar's leg. He felt an intense pain shooting through his right knee, and though he wanted to scream out, he held it in.

The Blaze lurched over and stood above the Purple Scar, his weapon aimed at the vigilante's head. The Purple Scar had a feeling that The Blaze would not be one to gloat over his near-victory, and that trying to talk to him would prove futile. He had to act, fast! The Purple Scar needed time to free his leg and, realizing that he would be unable to defeat The Blaze this night, he would have to make his getaway.

Time seemed to stand still as the Purple Scar saw The Blaze begin to depress the trigger of his flame thrower. There was only one chance to escape! The Purple Scar yanked his specialized pen out of his jacket and squeezed the trigger. A stream of black fluid leapt from the tip of his pen and onto The Blaze's welding mask. The dark liquid covered the transparent eyehole. The Blaze let go of the trigger, his hands going to his face in an attempt to clear his vision. The Purple Scar forced the box off his leg and hobbled away, feeling like a coward for retreating. Yet he had to accept the fact that tonight... he was unable to beat The Blaze.

As he made his way to his black sedan, the Purple Scar peeled off his mask in order to become Miles Murdock once more. The sounds of police sirens wailed in the distance, and Murdock breathed a sigh of relief. It was possible that someone heard the gunshots or saw The Blaze's fire. The Blaze had never confronted the police, so it was likely that he removed his armor to make his getaway. The situation in hand, Murdock drove back to his mansion.

The next morning, Murdock was sitting with Dale in his private study as he related the last night's events. She listen with rapt attention to the de-scription of The Blaze, and then felt a great a chill down her spine as Murdock told of his near death experience.

"Now I've got to figure out an explanation for why Miles Murdock would be walking with a limp... and find some way to stop The Blaze before he strikes again!" Murdock said bitterly with great frustration.

"Your leg could have been a simple accident. Falling down the stairs, maybe?" Dale said casually, before a stern look crossed her face. "But how to defeat The Blaze? It seems like short of dropping a bomb on him, nothing can stop him, Miles!"

Murdock thought of The Blaze once more, and though it was just a theory, he decided that he would voice it to Dale. "There are two things I can tell about The Blaze, at least psychologically..." he began "for one thing, he conceals his face. In my case, I designed my mask to strike fear into the hearts of the underworld and remind them of what they did to my brother. In his case the mask is plain, utilitarian... he is only concerned with killing and self-protection. He does not care to make an impression."

"His flames do that for him." Dale countered.

"True, but one other thing still bothers me. Every criminal, every *person* for that matter, has always shuddered at the sight of the Purple Scar. Yet he did not..." Murdock stopped, gathering his thoughts "...it means that he was expecting me... and since my appearance did not frighten him, he had seen me before! It keeps coming back to Alvin Shams. He was the only one who knew I was going to Roscoe's docks that night!"

"Miles, The Blaze is bigger than you are! Alvin is a small man!"

"Well..." Murdock began, but he could not think of a counter argument. Dale checked the ornate African clock on the wall and stood up quickly.

"Dr. Caldwell should be here any minute. I'll wait for him."

"Bring him here, Dale, please. It's only for a consultation after all, and since he's a survivor of one of The Blaze's attacks, I want to hear what he has to say."

Dale nodded as Murdock relaxed in his seat, trying to ignore the pain searing through his knee. He let his mind wander back to The Blaze's armor, and thought of its plated design. It must have been engineered to fold easily, possibly be stored in a portable container such as a large trunk. Thinking back, he remembered that The Blazes' hands rarely left his weapon. Were they somehow attached, or was arm movement difficult in that suit?

Before he could come to any conclusions, Dr. Caldwell walked into the office, accompanied by Dale. Murdock greeted him and motioned him towards the chair facing his desk. Caldwell looked uneasy as he sat down in the leather chair, doing his best to control his breathing. Murdock observed the burn wounds and singed flesh on Caldwell's face, and felt a great swell of pity for the man. Caldwell met Murdock's eyes and he began to talk nervously.

"I... well you can obviously guess why I'm here..." Caldwell said.

"Is something bothering you, Dr. Caldwell?" Murdock asked.

"Well... I'm just nervous about the surgery, that's all. I have a speech tonight and... and I'm afraid that they'll be looking at my scars, not hearing my words." Caldwell confessed. Murdock took an instant liking to the man. He was familiar with Caldwell's work, having read many of his medical journals and articles during his study of psychology.

"After the operation, you won't have to worry about a thing." Murdock said with a smile.

"No indeed! Dr. Murdock is one of the finest plastic surgeons in the country!" Dale said with pride in her voice as she stood by Murdock. Caldwell managed a half-hearted smile, but still seemed downcast.

"Yes, but there's still the matter of the bill. My research has cost a great deal and I have been forced to use my own money... I'm afraid that I have very little left." Caldwell admitted with a look of shame on his face. "I can't afford a man like you, Dr. Murdock. It was Elanor's... my wife's... idea."

"Dr. Caldwell, if I may be blunt, you barely escaped from The Blaze, correct?" Murdock said, straightening up. Caldwell thought back to the incident, and a disturbed look crossed his face which turned Murdock's stomach. He had seen war victims wear a similar expression, and he felt that innocent men did not deserve to suffer the same nightmares that he inflicted on the underworld.

"Yes, yes I did. It was the most terrifying night of my life... if you don't mind; I would rather not discuss it." Caldwell said with a mild, small voice, but his hand was gripping the arm rest of the chair tightly.

"I understand, but the point I was coming to was that, since you are a survivor of this awful ordeal... I will be treating you and all others injured by The Blaze free of charge."

"For... for free!" Caldwell said, his mouth agape. He looked to Dale, as if she would contradict the doctor, but she nodded encouragingly to Caldwell. "I can't believe it... this is wonderful, Dr. Murdock, I can scarcely believe that there still are men like you in the world. Men willing to forgo personal gain for the good of his fellow man." Caldwell was overwhelmed, and the words came sputtering out with relief and excitement.

"Dale mentioned that you are a psychologist..." Murdock said in an effort to calm Caldwell. There was still much to do in the day, and, as much as he wanted to have a conversation with Caldwell, he needed to keep moving.

"Oh yes, I am. I think I mentioned it earlier, but I'm giving a lecture tonight at Akelton University on emerging per...."

The phone rang, interrupting the psychologist. Murdock went to answer it, but Dale held up her hand, stopping him. She answered the phone while Murdock took Caldwell out into the hall to give Dale privacy. Murdock explained to Caldwell the specifics of his medical procedure and answered the few questions that he had. Murdock estimated that the burns were not too severe, and that Caldwell would, with the exception of a few minor marks, have a face that looked untouched.

While conversing with Caldwell, Murdock kept an ear on Dale's conversation. He gathered that it was Griffin, but could tell little more than that. Dale thanked the police captain for his efforts and hung up the phone. She walked into the hall and waved them back into Murdock's private office.

"It was Dan," Dale said, omitting Griffin's title, realizing that Caldwell would become suspicious if he knew that Murdock was in contact with the police. "He found the file you wanted on Mr. Shams, and can discuss it with you later."

"I see, thank you." Murdock said, now chomping at the bit to get in touch with Griffin. He noticed that Caldwell had perked up at the mention of Alvin's name.

"Tell me, are you referring to Alvin Shams?"

"Yes, he had consulted me earlier this week about getting a little cosmetic work done. Discreetly of course... why do you ask?" Murdock replied.

"It's just that he is, or rather was a patient of mine. I had not heard from him for some time, and I was wondering how he was getting on. Of course, I cannot say anything more than that. Client-patient confidentially, of course." Caldwell said quickly, realizing that he had already said too much.

He could not have estimated the importance of his words to Murdock. Murdock sat down in his chair once more. Handing the necessary paperwork to Caldwell, Murdock gave his usual consultation wrap-up speech. "Here is the paperwork detailing the procedures involved in the operation and Dale will help you set up an appointment. Now if you will excuse me, I have another patient arriving in..." Murdock turned to Dale, letting his sentence trail off.

"Mrs. Wood is coming in ten minutes, doctor." Dale said as she escorted Caldwell out of the office. The psychologist thanked him for his time and then left. When they were out of earshot, Murdock yanked the phone off its hook and dialed Griffin's private number as swiftly as he could. Ten minutes was not much time to talk between appointments, but he had to know more about Alvin Shams... especially considering that the man had been undergoing psychiatric treatment.

Griffin answered the phone with his usual professionalism, "Captain Dan Griffin," he said, identifying himself.

"It's me. Tell me about Alvin Shams and quickly! I only have a few minutes!" Murdock said urgently.

"There's not much to tell, to be honest..." Griffin said with a sigh "...he's got one speeding ticket from last year and paid the fine two days later. Other than that, he seems like a model citizen. I hate to break it to you, but I'm afraid that you're barking up the wrong tree yet again."

"It's him... it *has* to be him! He got caught in my trap last night! He either *is* The Blaze or *knows* The Blaze!" Murdock said in intense, but whispered tones. He could already hear Dale greeting his next patient at the door. To Murdock's chagrin, the woman was early.

"I understand how you feel, but there is no legal basis for investigation... unless the Purple Scar can unearth something else." Griffin suggested.

"The Purple Scar has already made himself known to Alvin... and The Blaze nearly killed him because of it. Maybe it's time for another player to enter the stage..." Murdock mused aloud, already thinking of another plan.

"Who?" said Griffin curiously.

"Oh... nobody."

That evening a plain, ordinary looking man in a tan overcoat walked towards the Grand Continental Railway building with a slight limp. He had a rather bland face, and no one would ever pick him out in a crowd. Murdock had sculpted the countenance deliberately that way for precisely that reason. In addition to his hideous Purple Scar mask, Miles Murdock had designed a nondescript face in order to continue his many investigations incognito. He limped due to his battle with The Blaze, and he hoped it would heal quickly. Speed was the only advantage that he held over his opponent, and Murdock could not afford to lose that.

The Grand Continental Railway was an impressive building. The building was not a train station, but rather the main railway office combined with a company museum. The structure was built of sturdy brick and mortar. Murdock observed various train cars on display, each accompanied by golden placards that gave detailed (if romanticized) versions of the railway's history. As his heels clacked on the tiled floor, Murdock looked around for the administrative office. Perhaps Alvin Shams' supervisor would be able to shed some light on his activities.

After being guided into his office by the secretary, Murdock (or rather Detective Baker as he was calling himself) was able to meet the head of the industrial designer and engineering teams. Tom Marvin was his name. He was middle-aged, but had an air of distinction about him. He kept his office as orderly and clean as his impeccable suit.

"I don't intend to take up much time, just a few minutes..." Murdock said as he sat down, taking out a pad of paper from his overcoat. He had used his fake police badge many times before, and playing a detective was becoming second nature to him.

"Anything at all to help the police." Tom said openly, but with a business-like sternness.

"Very well, sir. I have some questions about one of your employees, Mr. Alvin Shams."

"Shams? He's one of my best men! What could he have done?" Tom said with genuine astonishment. Clearly, Alvin was a respected and talented designer as far as his public persona went. His psychiatric treatment was probably a secret, Murdock thought.

"What can you tell me about him? Is he a good worker?"

"Oh yes, yes he is. One of our most brilliant engineers. A bit of a loner though, I admit. Is he in some sort of trouble?" Tom pressed, concerned with losing one of his best men.

"Has Mr. Shams been having any difficulty with his co-workers? Any reports of trouble?" Murdock said as he scribbled some notes on his pad.

"Well... a few of them have said he's been more aggressive lately. He seems to be more tired than usual and even snapped at me just the other day. He's normally a... a quiet man. I guess that he's been having some trouble with his latest assignment." Tom said, reflecting on the incidents involving Alvin.

"Has there been any unusual activity at the company? Any criminal activity?" Murdock said, ignoring Tom's questions. He certainly could not explain his theories about The Blaze to Tom, so he had to stick with asking questions yet providing no answers.

"Well... yes actually. Several months ago a large quantity of iron was stolen from one of our train depots. But we reported this to the police when it happened! There's been no progress whatsoever!" Tom said with a little indignation.

"Forgive me, sir. I was just assigned to this case. Iron seems an unusual thing to steal. It's not like you can sell it or..." Murdock said, thinking aloud. Of course, he figured that the iron stolen from the company was now The Blaze's armor.

"That's just what we thought. Nevertheless, it was stolen."

"Obviously, we have our leads and our theories, but do you *personally* have any suspects in mind?"

"Well I do... privately..." Tom said leaning in closer, as if not wanting to be overheard. "There is a man working for us at the depot in transportation. He often transports the iron and other supplies for our trains."

"His name?"

"Charlie Donovan... we have no proof of course, but I've always been suspicious of him. The only reason he has a job is because of his uncle. He..." Tom said, starting to go off on a tangent.

"Can you describe him?"

"Of course. Donovan's about five foot ten, fit, trim build. Brown hair, and a small scar on his left cheek." Tom said as he looked away from Murdock, as if trying to picture Charlie Donovan standing in the room.

"I never did like that man, but his uncle has tremendous influence with..."

Murdock did not have the time to listen, so he nodded politely and excused himself. Tom stood up, annoyed.

"Wait a minute!" the manager protested. "You haven't told me what all of this has to do with Alvin yet! I have a right to know! I'm his boss after all!"

Murdock slowed his opening of the door, but did not halt his motion completely as he answered, "When I get to the bottom of this, you'll be the first to know."

Driving in his black sedan, Murdock headed towards the train construction yard. The first purple shades of evening were beginning to creep across the sky, and Murdock knew that Donovan would be heading home soon. It was now or never, for each moment that Murdock spent away from The Blaze, the city was in danger.

Parking his sedan out of sight, Murdock walked towards the construction yard's parking lot. In the distance, he could hear the massive machinery of the construction yard grinding away. Sweaty workers hammered away on metal while rivets were added to the sides of train engines. Welding sparks illuminated various spots along the yard, while train engines and cars were assembled, coming to life in front of his eyes. The whole work yard had a feeling of lingering fatigue, probably because the work day was winding down. Murdock diverted his eyes from the construction yard and began looking at the cars in the parking lot.

Moments later, Murdock saw a man matching Charlie Donovan's description walking towards his car. He had a spring in his step, and a perpetually mischievous grin. Trailing him to his car, which was a slick, new model, (probably stolen or swindled, Murdock guessed) Murdock decided to make a bold move. Since it was a warm day, Donovan rolled down the windows of his car as he revved up the engine. Murdock reached into the passenger door and opened it from the inside.

"Hey! What do you think... What are you...?" Donovan began to stammer and shout. Murdock ignored him as he slid into the passenger seat. Pulling the .38 out of his pocket, Murdock casually rested his gun hand in his lap, aiming the weapon at Donovan's chest.

"If... if this is about the car. I swear I won it fair and square in a poker game with Gerald. There's no cause for this! I didn't cheat..." Donovan began, his mouth racing a mile a minute in fear.

"This isn't about your car..." Murdock said in slow, measured tones. He did not have time to check Donovan's criminal record with Griffin, but it was obvious he had underworld connections. Donovan would logically be more frightened of rival criminals than a police officer, so Murdock decided that he would be playing the role of a hood now. "...it's about that iron you stole."

"Wha...? Iron? How do you know about that?" Donovan said, confused and surprised.

"I know... what I need to know is why you stole it." Murdock said, but he could tell that Donovan was in no mood to reveal anything further. In fact, his smile betrayed his arrogance.

"Listen mister, I can tell you're new at this. If only one man can tell you what you need to know, you don't threaten to shoot him. That's just plain stupid. And furthermore..."

Suddenly, Donovan lunged at him! His talking was only a distraction to keep Murdock off guard. The gun dropped to the floor while the two struggled in the car. Donovan, ever the coward, was trying to escape, but Murdock was gripping his shirt with an unbreakable grasp. It was true; he could not risk harming Donovan because he desperately needed the information. However, in his current condition, Donovan could easily outpace Murdock on foot. He had to find a way to subdue him in the car.

Donovan, though, was free from any such inhibitions. He grabbed Murdock by the face, digging his nails into his false skin. Donovan yanked his hands away, and was greeted by the shock of his life! He would have torn deeply into the skin of a normal man, but since Murdock had been wearing his "plain face", Donovan had torn it off completely! Underneath that mask was not the face of Miles Murdock, but the face of the Purple Scar!

"Oh my god..." Donovan said, his breath taken away.

The Purple Scar knocked the mask out of Donovan's hands and grabbed him by the collar. Leaning in close, to maximize the effect of the shock, the Purple Scar yelled in Donovan's face.

"The iron you stole is now being used by The Blaze! Who paid you to steal it?"

Donovan was still in shock, and the Purple Scar needed answers. Though it was not a medically sound method, it was the only option he had. Striking Donovan back and forth across the face, the Purple Scar demanded his answer once more.

"Who needed the iron?"

"That little guy... Shams... Alvin Shams..." Donovan managed to get out. "He... he gave me all the money he had... but he said that he really wanted the iron... I don't know why..."

"Oh, my god....!"

"You're a fool, Donovan!" The Purple Scar raged at him. "He used that iron to become The Blaze! You're just as responsible for the fires as he is!"

"What? How was I supposed to know he was going to do that?" Donovan said with a pleading look in his eyes, his voice trembling. "One day he's this quiet, little man, and the next he's acting like a lunatic! I was frightened of him, honest! I did what he said, no questions asked! I swear that he was going to kill me!"

The Purple Scar had a difficult time imagining that anyone could have been frightened of Alvin Shams. Still, one look at the quivering, terrified man next to him told him that Donovan was telling the truth. If Donovan, a man who had a history with organized crime, was afraid of Alvin, then there was a side to him that nobody, save for Dr. Caldwell, might know. Nevertheless, the Purple Scar had what he needed out of Donovan.

"Good night."

The Purple Scar raised a fist to strike Donovan into unconsciousness, but he was too late. Donovan had fainted. Releasing his grip on him, the Purple Scar made a mental note to tell Griffin about Donovan later. Right now, his top priority was to discover The Blaze's location and save lives.

Driving through the city that night, Miles Murdock turned on his windshield wipers as heavy fists of rain began to hammer on his car. If The Blaze decided to come out that night, he would be at a major disadvantage. The rain would counteract the effect of the flames, and he would have difficulty walking on wet ground. It would almost compensate for the damaged knee that Murdock was struggling with. He was driving to Dale Jordan's home, for he agreed to be her companion for Dr. Caldwell's lecture at Akelton University. She thought that the two of them (and especially Murdock, being knowledgeable about psychology) would enjoy the lecture on theoretical science. Murdock thought it would be a good opportunity to talk to the doctor afterwards about Alvin Shams.

A great deal was on his mind, and Murdock began to sift through the facts as he drove in silence. Alvin Shams was a brilliant engineer and designer who had recently become antisocial and angry. He was seeing a therapist, obviously in secret, to possibly combat this problem. Though it was hasty to make a positive diagnosis, Murdock believed that Alvin Shams suffered from a dual personality disorder. One was the meek man that the Purple Scar had interrogated, and the other was The Blaze! That explained, to Murdock, why he could not detect any signs of Alvin Shams lying... to his knowledge he truly had not committed any crimes. It was The Blaze who was behind the string of arsons... but why? He would need to consult with Dr. Caldwell on that matter, but he had thought he worked out another problem: his armor.

How did a small, physically unimpressive man like Alvin fit inside the metal contraption that he had built for himself? Then Murdock realized that an engineer as brilliant as Shams, who would be capable of creating collapsible armor, would have been able to fabricate a system of arm and leg extensions in order to disguise his height. His flamethrower was obviously of his own design as well, and it explained why he rarely moved his hands from it. With the arm extensions, Alvin had to keep the fingers in a locked position. It would have been quite a struggle to move.

As Murdock turned down another street, he thought of the two most important questions that were bothering him: why was The Blaze killing random people, and how could he defeat him? He pulled up outside of Dale's house, where she was waiting patiently, and the two sped off into the night.

Dale was wearing a blue dress that Murdock had bought her last Christmas, and she looked absolutely stunning. When Dale got into the passenger's seat, Murdock was at a loss for words. She smiled at him, a look of quiet contentment on her face.

"Thank you very much, Miles. That means a lot coming from you."

"But I didn't say anything..." he said, wondering what she meant.

"If I can distract Miles Murdock, A.K.A. The Purple Scar from his brooding, then I must really look like something special tonight!"

"That you do." said Murdock as they made their way down Swank Street. "I now know that without a shadow of a doubt, that Alvin Shams is The Blaze. I just don't know why he's burning down buildings... and I have *no* idea how to beat him! Any thoughts?"

"Well..." Dale began, looking out the window as she thought aloud "... maybe these attacks are not random. He could be going after specific people..."

"Wouldn't it be easier to shoot them?" Murdock countered.

"But you're thinking as how *you* would solve the problem. Alvin Shams is clearly a pyromaniac, and for him, this would be his preferred method."

"But what about the collateral damage? And all of the innocent people?"

"I don't think he cares," Dale said with a grim expression on her face.

"But why?" Murdock said aloud. He found himself agreeing with Dale, but still could not work out a motive for the assaults. Murdock explained to Dale his theory of Alvin's split personality with The Blaze, and the workings of his armor.

"I think that we can get Dr. Caldwell to talk. Who knows? Perhaps it will tie in with his lecture on emerging personalities." Dale said optimistically.

"Emerging personalities! Good god why didn't I realize that before! That's why The Blaze is murdering people! The Blaze is trying to take complete control of Alvin! He's killing everyone that could possibly help Alvin defeat him!" Murdock said with a rush of excitement.

"But who? He's killed scores of people in Akelton City!"

"Just as long as he got his target! You're right, Dale! He's been targeting specific people... just like I accused Roscoe of doing! I wouldn't be surprised when Griffin interviews the victim's families and cross references them, he'll find at least one person that was a friend or acquaintance of Alvin Shams."

"I see your point..." Dale said. She looked out the window to see that the buildings were speeding by unusually fast. Turning to Murdock, Dale saw that his knuckles were white. The familiar lines at the corners of his mouth and above his right eye made their appearance. They always surfaced when he was in a state of deep, intense concentration.

"What is it?" Dale asked with great concern.

"I know where The Blaze is going to be tonight! He'll be trying to burn down the Akelton University lecture hall to kill Dr. Caldwell. It fits his profile of trying to cover his tracks. One murder amongst a series of murders!"

"And with Dr. Caldwell as his therapist... he'd be The Blaze's number one target!" Dale exclaimed.

"He was lucky to escape with his life the first time..." Murdock said as he turned a sharp corner. "The Blaze won't make the same mistake this time. He'll hunt him down like a dog unless the Purple Scar can get there first!"

"But do you have any idea how you are going to stop him? You just finished telling me that you had nothing that could put a dent in him... not to mention that you're hurt." Dale cautioned.

"I'll have to think of something when I get there." Murdock said. He was not attempting a show of bravado; that was the only plan that came to his mind at the moment.

+++

Under ordinary circumstances, driving to Akelton University would have been a delight to Miles Murdock. However, now was not the time for nostalgia. The older buildings, looking more like European cathedrals than modern educational facilities, resembled gothic paintings as the rain came down. The vast campus, normally a pleasant memory of bygone days to Murdock, was now a source of frustration. He had no idea where The Blaze could be hiding, and he did not have time to search. Getting to Dr. Caldwell and safely evacuating the lecture hall was their mission.

The campus had not changed too much since he had last been there, and he was able to drive to the lecture hall parking lot almost from memory. Dale indicated to a small poster propped in front of the doors that read: "Emerging Personalities: An Astounding Lecture by Dr. Phillip Caldwell."

Racing out of the car, Dale ran out into the pouring rain and under the entrance's shelter. Murdock trailed slightly behind; his knee was not cooperating.

"What do we do?" Dale asked as she pushed her hair out of her face.

"Obviously The Blaze isn't here yet. So we need to warn Caldwell and…" Murdock's attention was diverted by an unusual sight. He had been quickly observing the cars in the parking lot as he limped to the lecture hall. The majority of the cars were classy, expensive looking vehicles. The kind of car that a successful doctor or scientist would drive. He counted on seeing many of that type there, but one car in particular caught his attention.

It was an older yellow car, standing in sharp contrast to the rest of the slick, polished new ones. The yellow car did not belong there, and acting on instinct, Murdock ran as fast he could towards it. Dale called after him.

"Miles, where are you going?" she demanded.

"Get to the lecture hall and warn everyone! The Blaze is here!"

Dale nodded and pushed open the door to the lecture hall, running inside with a determined look etched across her face. Murdock knew that he could focus more with Dale handling the crowd. Pulling out his set of master keys, Murdock forced his way into the yellow car and hastily examined it with his pencil flashlight. He noticed distinctive impressions and scuffs on the passenger seat. They were in the shape of a square, as if a large trunk had left permanent indentations.

Murdock also spied a crumpled piece of paper left lying underneath the brake pedal. Picking it up, he quickly unfolded it and saw a list of names, written with a harsh, deranged hand. All of them had been scratched out viciously. The only exception was "Phillip Caldwell", which *was* scratched out, but later circled multiple times. That was clearly the moment when The Blaze realized that his target was still alive.

Pocketing the note, Murdock had to cut his investigation short. The Blaze was already moving into position, and the Purple Scar was the only hope they had! Reaching into the secret pocket of his coat, Murdock once more donned the mask to become the Purple Scar. Studying the ground around him for tracks, it was impossible to tell which direction Alvin had been heading, but when the Purple Scar moved to examine the grassy field next to the parking lot, he saw that some ground had been kicked up... Alvin was dragging the cumbersome trunk to his destination.

The Purple Scar ran after him, cursing his injured knee. It had slowly started to heal, but it was still a detriment to him. Following the trail around the campus, he hoped that luck would be on his side and he would catch Alvin before he became The Blaze. Based on the tracks he had left, Alvin had discovered the lecture hall's side entrance, and was going to take Dr. Caldwell by surprise. The Purple Scar had to catch himself from slipping on the soaking wet grass as the trail started to wind down.

Unfortunately for the Purple Scar, Alvin was gone, and The Blaze stood before him. The rain cascaded down his armor, while the lights from the university buildings caused The Blaze to resemble a hideous distortion of a medieval knight. His back was to the Purple Scar as he stalked towards the lecture hall. The Blaze was also having difficulty not slipping in the rain, more than the Purple Scar because of the immense weight he was carrying. The Purple Scar thought to use that to his advantage.

He knew it would be ineffective to shoot, but it would catch The Blaze's attention. The Purple Scar pulled out his .38 revolver and fired into The Blaze's gas tank. Once more, the bullets sparked harmlessly off his armor, but the lumbering giant turned around to face the Purple Scar.

"You..." The Blaze said menacingly.

"Stop this, Alvin!" the Purple Scar yelled, "You need help! You've been murdering innocent people!"

"Innocent? They want me dead!" The Blaze yelled as he shot a stream of fire at the Purple Scar. The vigilante dived out of harm's way, but his knee sent him whiplashes of pain. The Purple Scar did his best to disguise his wound, but he could not keep this up much longer.

"Alvin! No one is after you! They want to help you!" The Purple Scar yelled.

"Alvin? He is gone! I am The Blaze!" the monstrous voice declared through his mask. "All my life, I wanted in... I wanted control! Alvin was a waste of life! Mocked and spurned because of his weakness! He tried to forget me... forget the fires I made for him! The beautiful fire! All his life, those who wronged Alvin would burn! I was protecting him... and how did he repay me? He tried to kill me! He told all those people about my beautiful fires! Why was I protecting him? I should have been protecting myself!"

"You are Alvin! Don't you realize that?

"Alvin is weak... do I look weak to you, Purple Scar! I am what Alvin *should* have been!" Deciding that the conversation was over, The Blaze leveled his flamethrower at the Purple Scar once more. "You will also burn this night, Purple Scar!"

The Purple Scar knew what was coming, and made a desperate gamble. It was futile to attempt a long-distance battle with The Blaze, for his flamethrower could outreach anything the Purple Scar had. Instead, he ran headlong at The Blaze, ignoring the sharp pains in his knee. The Blaze blasted another jet of orange flames at him, but the Purple Scar slid underneath it, looking like a baseball player sliding into home. Riding along on the wet grass, he stopped close to The Blaze's legs and used a jiu-jitsu leg takedown to bring the metal titan crashing to the earth.

Climbing on top of The Blaze, the Purple Scar tried feverishly to remove his helmet. However, the Purple Scar was so focused on his task that he failed to see The Blaze had let go of the weapon with his left hand. The Blaze swung his free arm with all of his might, clobbering the Purple Scar like an iron baseball bat.

Flying off The Blaze and landing some distance away, the Purple Scar had to focus, for he was seeing double! The Blaze had taken great efforts to rise to a kneeling position. His left hand grasped the flamethrower again, and the Purple Scar hobbled across the grass as he was pursued by another geyser of flame.

Racing against the flame, the Purple Scar saw his only chance at survival in front of him: a car. He yanked out his pistol again and fired, blowing out a window as he climbed in. He looked up to see The Blaze back on his feet again, menacingly walking towards the Purple Scar. The vigilante gathered his thoughts, trying to think of his next move. The Blaze, however, gave him no quarter. He set the car ablaze with an onslaught of flames. The Purple Scar ducked the blast, but the car was now burning around him! He thought about jumping out, but his knee was throbbing with such intensity that he decided against it. The Purple Scar would have to plan each movement carefully.

Suddenly, he seized upon an idea. With the car melting around him, it was only a matter of time before the gas tank caught fire and exploded!

Hastily, the Purple Scar reached underneath the steering wheel and quickly hotwired the ignition. It roared to life, and the Purple Scar slammed the pedal to the floor.

The Purple Scar went careening into The Blaze with his flaming wreck of a car. Despite his great strength and size, The Blaze was knocked to the earth when struck by the tremendous force. The Purple Scar kept the car moving forward and parked on top of the metal titan, pinning him underneath. By now, the Purple Scar could feel his skin burning, his mask starting to melt, and feared that his clothes were about to catch fire.

Kicking the door open with his good leg, the Purple Scar ran away from the burning car as swiftly as he was able. The Purple Scar was knocked to the earth by the thundering explosion that followed seconds later. It was accompanied by another powerful blast, and the Purple Scar turned around in time to see that it was The Blaze's gas tank that blew. Consumed in a fireball, The Blaze, who had taken over the body of Alvin Shams, was no more.

Mrs. Elanor Caldwell greeted Dale and Murdock with a charming smile and a hearty handshake. She was quite the elegant lady, and it was easy to see why Dr. Caldwell thought the world of her. They met at the front door of Murdock's estate, and she presented him with a slim, leather-bound volume of Dr. Caldwell's latest paper.

"You've made my husband look like his old self again. Thank you, Dr. Murdock, and you too, Miss Jordan!" she said as she pressed the volume into his hand. She then shook Dale's hand with great enthusiasm.

"You're welcome—you know, psychology has always fascinated me," Murdock said as he looked at the book. "Is it a copy of his lecture? I was sorry that it was so dramatically...postponed."

"Well, ever since the Purple Scar left that statement for the press about The Blaze's real identity, my husband... well, it validated all of his claims. He was walking on cloud nine!" Mrs. Caldwell said with pride in her voice. Dale looked at Murdock with a satisfied smile.

"I suppose that there has been only one downside to this whole affair," Mrs. Caldwell admitted, though judging by the smile on her face, it was obvious that the consequence was not too terrible.

"What is it?" Dale asked.

"Now my husband has become obsessed with the Purple Scar! When Miss Jordan escorted him away, my husband caught a glimpse of his battle with The Blaze! Now he's been concocting all kinds of wild theories and notions about him! He's determined to make a thorough psychological study of the Purple Scar. What you have here is what he's been working on so far."

"I think that will make very interesting reading, don't you think, Doctor?" Dale said. Though it would be undetectable to any one who did not know her, Murdock knew that Dale was teasing him.

"Yes, I'll read through it tonight." Murdock said sincerely.

"Well good luck, I have not had a chance to edit it yet. His writing is very... well let's just say that he needs me," Mrs. Caldwell said with a sly grin.

They thanked her and she walked away from them, happily going to meet her husband for lunch. Dale leaned over and looked curiously at the leather book. Opening up the cover, she skimmed over the contents and a sour expression came across her beautiful face.

"Well *that's* gratitude for you!" she said as she pointed to the heading.

Murdock looked down to where Dale was pointing.

"The Madness of the Purple Scar..." Murdock read aloud, amused.

In truth, he was grateful for Dr. Caldwell's hasty assessment of the Purple Scar. Murdock had worked tirelessly to achieve the Purple Scar's reputation as an ever present nightmare among the criminal class, and now that a professional had declared him insane... Murdock could not help but feel successful.

THE END

THE HORROR HERO

To be perfectly honest, Airship 27, for me, has introduced a great number of characters and crime fighters that I was unaware existed... and boy was it my loss! Take the Purple Scar for example. No sooner do I start writing for Airship 27, then before I see the book cover for their first volume of him. I know the phrase is "never judge a book by it's cover", but it was sure hard not to... I loved it! Thus, I made a mental note to write a tale for him one day.

When I inquired about writing a Purple Scar tale, Ron told me to play up the horror aspects of the character. That concept stuck in my head, keeping the story in the horror realm. I took inspiration in one of the genre's most classic villains, Mr. Hyde, for the character of The Blaze. I was interested in replicating the physical and mental transformation (from Jekyll to Hyde), but not through chemical processes. Rather, I looked to the opposite side of the scientific spectrum to find inspiration in the technological. To me, most of the pulp heroes are incredible he-men, so when you place an opponent that can dominate them in the story, the hero is forced to use his brains, and the story then becomes much more interesting.

I was also intent in exploring the concept of a hero's hunch not panning out. I strongly doubt that I am the first writer to attempt this, but it's something new for me. I found it interesting to have a hero who is as nearly flawless as Miles Murdock (seriously, the man is an expert in everything he attempted) be flat out wrong. Instead of blindly following the hero, the side characters can now express a healthy amount of doubt, as one does when concerned for a friend.

Reading through the character bible, the Purple Scar struck me as one of the grizzliest heroes in the pulp world, so I had to step outside my comfort zone a bit (it is a very large comfort zone I admit) in order to understand how he would deal with criminals. Most heroes have boundaries and would generally prefer not to fight in order to solve a problem. Yet, I sensed that Murdock had a dark, uncontrollable anger within him, and actually relished in dispatching his foes, though not in the sadistic sense. I also felt a need to make the action scenes a little less superhero in feeling (the Purple Scar is actually injured in a battle, as opposed to walking it off like the majority of heroes), and the peril should be much more frightening.

I hope you have enjoyed this story, because I had a great deal of difficulty in finding a way to finally kill The Blaze. I suppose if I could ever presume to give any writer any advice, it would be to make sure your villains are somehow killable!

+++

ERIK FRANKLIN - is a writer/actor/filmmaker based in Seattle. Recently graduating with honors from the Art Institute of Seattle in film production, he is the co-President of Franklin-Husser Entertainment LLC. He is working on two upcoming feature films for his company: A dinosaur action film "Revenge of the Lost" and the martial arts comedy "3 Morons Fighting Ninja". You can give the company page a "Like" at: https://www.facebook.com/pages/Franklin-Husser-Entertainment-LLC/290795021042906.

Drawn to pulp fiction through his love of history, literature, and Americana, he is grateful for Airship 27 Productions giving him the opportunity to write his first story. He looks forward to writing more adventures!

THE DEADLY DOPPLEGANGER!

BY DAVID NOE

"Tommy!"

He was used to people screaming his name. He'd heard it all his life from one person and another. It was usually in anger or disappointment, almost never in astonishment or happy greetings. He got to the point where even he didn't like his name sometimes. That's why he made a habit of changing it so often.

"Tommy, wake up!"

The funny thing was, he wasn't even sleeping. He was going to a party. That's what he remembered, anyway. There was this swanky uptown party with Dale and Mr. Murdock. Yeah, and there was a guy pretending to be someone else… the Purple Scar!

"Come on, Tommy. There's not much time."

Tommy was well acquainted with being someone else. It was his shell game for years. He was the ultimate con man, able to slip into the role of another person, able to get away from the real world, from the troubles and the poverty and the people screaming his name.

"Tommy!"

They could scream at the other people, the people he pretended to be. It didn't matter what happened to them, even if it landed him in jail. He could always be someone else. This worked out swell for him, well, swell enough. It wasn't like he was ever going to be anybody anyway. If he kept on inventing new people to be, maybe one of them would stick. Maybe one of them would be his ticket out of this depression that the world suffered. It looked like there wasn't any future for anybody anymore. The American dream was a nightmare that nobody would ever wake up from.

"Open your eyes, Tommy."

That was before the Purple Scar, before Miles Murdock came into his life and gave him a chance. Mr. Murdock let him in on the biggest secret, the biggest con against the criminal world. It was eye opening. He couldn't believe it.

"It's Miles, Tommy. Are you okay?"

Miles Murdock was the Purple Scar. He fought the underworld with a vengeance that was otherworldly. He was a hurricane of justice with the face of a corpse. Tommy could still feel the shiver down his spine as Doctor Miles Murdock was transformed into the hideous creature, merely by donning an expertly crafted mask, likened after the doctor's murdered, scarred and abandoned brother. Tommy still felt the trickle of sweat on his brow and the knot in his stomach as the Purple Scar approached him. His heart pounded in his ears as the shadowy protector of Akelton City got closer and closer.

"Tommy," the Purple Scar's voice wafted on the cold breeze, "Tommy, open your eyes..."

And then, he grabbed him. Tommy jolted awake. Pebbles skittered away under his feet. The setting sun cast long shadows on the hillside above him. His eyes darted in circles as he madly tried to make sense of his surroundings, the stone outcropping on which he sat, the baseball sized stone on his lap and the desperate hands of a man in black pants and a white dress shirt grabbing him by the shoulders.

"Aaah!" Tommy nearly fell over the rocky cliff. He was sweating and his head hurt. He waved his hands and knocked the round stone off his lap, but the stern hands of his friend held tightly to him and wouldn't let him fall.

"It's okay! I've got you," the authoritative voice of Miles Murdock immediately calmed Tommy enough that he was able to get his bearings.

"The car!" Tommy looked to the shadows.

"It's on the other side of this boulder," Miles had his leg wrapped around a sapling while he reached out from a very narrow ridge to grasp Tommy, "We were thrown free, but I think Dale is still in it."

"My head hurts," Tommy struggled to get up.

"I'll examine it as soon as we get you some place more stable." Miles pulled up on Tommy's jacket, "That ledge won't support you much longer. Come along, now."

"Whoa, I..." Tommy's legs wobbled beneath him as he tried to focus on the line of darkness below him, "I can't move, Mr. Murdock! I keep telling my legs to go, but they won't listen to me. Oh my gosh, that's a long way down!"

A chunk of ground pulled away beneath his feet and he fell back out of Miles' grasp. It busted up into little pieces as it bounced all the way down the cliff.

"You can do it, Tommy," Miles' voice was calm, but firm, "You've done better than this before. Think about those close calls that you sailed right through."

Tommy remembered the wild bomber he talked down during the Hovering Skull case. He was just a button push away from death. He was able to convince that crazy Bolshevik to stand down while the Purple Scar took down the Manx. He looked over to Miles. The doctor stood there, hands out, blood running down his arm through a rip in his shirt, his dark purple tie flapping like a flag in the cold wind. Tommy recalled the Hyperion Score when they were outnumbered by Chelsea's Gang of Idiots. Tommy had half of them fighting on his side before the Purple Scar was able to figure out the jimmied switch on the boxcar. Tommy swallowed hard and straightened his own checkered bow tie. He took a deep breath and stood fully, looking only into the determined eyes of his friend and mentor. He never looked down, never looked away until his hand was firmly in the strong capable hands of the master plastic surgeon. Then, he made his mistake. He looked away and the ground deceived him.

"Woaaaaaa!" Tommy fell away from the crumbling cliff.

Miles grunted and grabbed at him with his other hand. "Huff!" He swept across in an arc, holding himself to the wall with his legs wrapped around the bowed sapling.

Tommy flew like an errant kite into the outcropping on the other side of the boulder. He landed in a pile of sand. Miles released him and grabbed on to the tall weeds and limbs to keep himself from falling. He pulled himself up, and they both sat on the sandy soil, panting. Tommy put his head in his hands. Below them, the rushing sounds of Sand Arch Creek swallowed up the soil and stones the men fed it.

"I got a headache," Tommy said.

"No doubt," Miles stood, "Now we know your head isn't quite as hard as a rock."

Tommy held up his hand to accept Miles' help getting up, but the doctor was gone. He had leapt a small crevice and was even now sprinting towards the once pristine dark red 1939 Lincoln Zephyr convertible that balanced, nose in the air, about a hundred yards away in the dusky distance. The top was down, and Tommy could see the unconscious figure of Dale slumped back in the front seat.

"Dale!" Miles yelled, "I'm coming!"

Tommy stood and dusted his pants off. He once again tightened his bow tie. He sniffed and addressed the crevice in front of him. One of the early memories he had of the young nurse, Dale Jordan, was of her leaping, only he was the obstacle. He was lying on the concrete floor of a greasy old warehouse, fighting a bunch of fake pirates with the Purple Scar. One of them had landed a solid blow, and had knocked him down with a bloody nose. Dale jumped out of the shadows where she wasn't even supposed to be, and ran towards the Scar.

"Hello?" Tommy said to her. "Bleeding here?"

When the Purple Scar saw her, he whipped into action double time. By the time she reached him, the last pirate was hitting the floor.

"I came to help," she looked up at the monstrous Scar and never even flinched.

"You should have stayed home," Miles' voice still held an edge of the creepiness of the Purple Scar, "You could get hurt."

"You'll save me," she touched his chest, "You always do. I can't help it if I'm falling…"

Tommy jumped with all of his determination and made it just far enough not to be claimed by the gravity of the cliff. It was far enough for him.

The last few strides, Miles nearly flew. It was like in his college days, when the goal line was in sight, his leaps covered great distances. He was a bird taking wing. He was an airplane preparing to take off. He came down on the trunk of the car with a weight that rocked it backwards. The jolt startled Dale into consciousness.

"Wha… What?" she instinctively grabbed her purse and looked around at the incredible panorama of the horizon. The top of the convertible was down, and it let in quite a view. She placed her hand to her mouth to stifle a scream. She had learned that screaming almost never improved a situation. Many times it put her and the Purple Scar into greater danger.

"Dale," Miles inched forward until the car started creaking on the balance, "Come this way. Crawl over the seat."

"That was the Purple Scar," Dale turned around to Miles She had a swelling around her eye that would be quite a shiner if she lived long enough, "The Purple Scar ran us off the road. That's…"

"I know," Miles held out his hand, "Let's get you out of this car."

Dale turned in the seat. Every movement was met with an equal squeal or creak of protest from the car and the loose rocks. She pulled her long auburn hair out of her face. The wind whipped locks were blinding her. She tied it in a quick knot and raised up to climb over. Immediately, the car shifted.

"Oh!" she cried.

"Reach out!" Miles wished he could stretch his arms and grab her.

"I'm on it!" Tommy jumped up on the bumper and leveled the car, "Grab 'er quick!"

Miles and Dale fell towards one another. He pulled her up and twisted them both out the side of the car. They landed in the grass at the right edge of the cliff. Their legs dangled over the precipice, but they held to each other for an extra moment, just to make sure they were both safe.

"Holy cats!" Tommy sat down on the trunk, "That was very nearly a close one. What are we gonna do now?"

Miles leapt up, startling Tommy. Tommy hopped off the car as it began to tip downward.

"My coat!" Miles jumped into the back seat as the vehicle slid towards the depths.

"Whoa!" Tommy grabbed the bumper and pulled, but the weight had shifted beyond any salvation. The bumper ripped free of his grasp, and he fell over backwards into the scrub.

"Miles!" Dale scrambled up.

As the car scraped free of the cliff, Miles threw his coat and doctor bag back over the end of the car. He placed his foot on the back of the seat as the automobile became airborne, and he leapt with all the strength in his athletic frame. Even still, it was less like he actually jumped up than like the car fell away. For a fraction of a second, it was as if he could reach out and grab the cliff, or the grass and roots or anything, really, to save himself, to keep himself from tumbling down into the inky rapids with the Zephyr, but only for a fraction of a second. Then, it was obvious that he could not. It was too late at last. He just didn't have the reach.

His life didn't flash before his eyes. He would have plenty of time for that on the way down. He thought, instead of his brother, the proud honest cop, gunned down and savaged before his time. He thought of his mission to stop the kind of vermin that caused it. It was a consuming thought, and it got him through many difficult times, times that focused that anger and that zeal into his fists and his persona, but now he had nothing to hit. Now, he reached out into nothing, thinking perhaps that was all he had left.

"Hupff!" Tommy grabbed one of Miles' hands with both of his.

"Haaakk!" Dale grabbed his other hand.

They both fell flat to the ground as Miles' weight jerked them down into the rocks. They gritted their teeth and held tight, dangling over the cliff with only their bottom half on solid earth. Dale panted and closed her eyes. Tommy pulled himself up to a seated position. In a moment, they had pulled Miles up with them into the grass. They all lay there, huffing. Miles turned over onto his back and looked up at the first stars of the evening. The Zephyr crashed into the rocks below and was as quiet as the night around them. They all sat in silence until the crickets started up again.

"I quite liked that auto," Miles said at last.

"It was a swell rig. That's for sure," Tommy smiled.

Dale swept at her dress and frowned. "My evening gloves were in the glove compartment," she said.

"Want me to go fetch 'em?" Tommy grinned.

The three of them laughed for a moment and began to rise. They patted at each other to knock loose some of the grass and sand and rocks from their ruined evening wear.

"This will have to do," Dale smiled and untied her hair, "I think I have a brush in my purse. It's over here somewhere."

"She held onto her purse," Tommy turned to Miles and pointed his thumb at Dale, "Dames!"

"Indeed," Miles rolled up his sleeve, revealing a long narrow cut, "Thankfully, I gathered my own bag, as well."

"Holy cats, Doc," Tommy grabbed Miles' arm, "That's a doozy."

"It's mostly stopped bleeding," Miles held it up to the last of the light, "I can get it cleaned and bandaged. I don't think it's very deep."

"Still and all…" Tommy said.

"That's tonight, then," Dale dug through her small bag. She took great pride in all that she could stuff into the purse, but it made finding things a chore, "Now we need to find a way home."

"I think not," Miles knelt down and opened his bag and examined the topsy turvy mess, "My goodness."

"You got a plan?" Tommy picked up a hubcap that the Zephyr had lost.

"I have a party," Miles said, "We have a party to attend. Let us go see who is surprised we made it."

"Oh!" Dale exclaimed to a compact mirror.

"What is it?" Miles dropped his bag and stood.

"I'm going to have a black eye!" Dale pouted, "I do believe I am going to have a shiner!"

"Let me look at it," Miles pulled a small flashlight from his bag.

"Don't you dare," Dale turned away and pulled out a powder brush and swept it across her high cheekbone, "I'll not be seen in this manner. I can cover it with makeup."

"I am a doctor, remember?" Miles put his hand on her shoulder, "Besides, I've seen a lot worse and a lot more of a lot of people."

Dale hung her head and turned around. She stuck out her lower lip and lowered her shoulders.

"Good Lord!" Miles said.

"What? Is it that bad?" Dale opened her eyes in shock.

Miles smiled and pulled her close. He laughed quietly.

"Oh, you!" Dale pushed away and frowned.

Miles laughed out loud, "I was just…"

"Give me that," Dale snatched the light and stomped off into the weeds, "You are a thoughtless oaf."

"Don't you think you should wait until we climb back up the hill before you get all made up again?" Tommy called off to her.

"You too!" Dale called from the darkness.

"Me?" Tommy walked up to Miles, "I didn't do nothin'."

"Never cross Jordan," Miles said.

"Brother, don't I know it," Tommy rubbed his temple.

"How is your head?" Miles put his hands on his hips and looked off into the shadows.

"Still on my shoulders," Tommy polished the hub cap with his elbow, "and throbbing like the Dickens."

Miles sat on a rock and pulled some gauze from his bag. "Good thing I keep the alcohol wrapped up. Even so, I'm surprised it survived the experience."

"You and me both, pal," Tommy took the gauze Miles handed to him, "I'm surprised any thing or anybody survived the experience. Of course, surviving the experience is something we've become old pros at."

"Still, I wish Dale hadn't been here," Miles uncorked the brown bottle of alcohol, "I hate it when she is in danger."

"You know, I was wondering," Tommy handed the gauze back to Miles, "Who knew we were coming to this shindig?"

"More importantly… sssssss…" Miles tightened his lips and hissed as he cleaned his wound, "Why would they want to kill us for it? As far as Carlisle is concerned, we're just coming to his party as political donors. You'd think he would want to see us get there and write him a big fat check."

"It's gonna take a lot of dough to beat Mayor Crenshaw," Tommy winced at Miles wincing, "Besides, I thought this fake Purple Scar was working for Carlisle."

"I'll see that murderous scum taken out before he causes any more death," Miles clenched the fist of his wounded arm and threw the bloody gauze into his bag, "even if he's just killing criminals. No one gets away with killing in my name... not in my town."

The long cut on the inside of Miles forearm was mostly dry as he applied a bandage and taped it down. Tommy had become adept at helping with the field dressings. They had both seen too many close shaves with instruments of all dangerous sizes. It was a supernatural force that kept Miles returning to the fray over and over. That same grit earned him a horrible legend of being nearly indestructible, of being able to reach into the spirit realm, of perhaps not being entirely human. As the fear of the Scar grew, it was lost on many that never had the Scar taken a life. Miles allowed that fear to grow for the purpose of aiding his battle, and Tommy found his way into the dark dens of the underworld on many occasions to scour for information and to spread the dread. There were many nights, though, that Miles, and even Tommy, had been saved by their own Florence Nightingale. Dale was invaluable to the team, even if Miles was reticent to admit it. She was skilled beyond her years, and had had to master medical skills that she should not ever have had to do. Miles taught her well. They worked well together.

"I don't think you are even necessary," Dale stood beside Tommy and looked down on Miles. In the dim light, her swollen cheek was barely noticeable, except for the fact that her eye was swelling shut, "Perhaps I should be the plastic surgeon."

"Um..." Tommy pointed to his own eye.

"Very good, Dale," Miles tapped Tommy's leg, "Right, Tommy?"

"Oh, you can't fool me," Dale stomped her foot, "I look hideous."

"No, I was..." Miles rolled down his sleeve.

"I'm sure it, uh..." Tommy pulled at his tie.

"Hello?" a voice called from up on the road.

"Oh, thank God," Miles said, "Hello?"

"Ya'll alright down there?" the voice of the shadowy figure said, "I heard a ruckus and came to check it out? Everybody okay?"

"We're okay, mister," Tommy cupped his mouth.

"Can ya' walk? Do I need ta' come down there?"

"I think we..."

"I got an old rope that'll reach part of the way," the man up top said, "Hold on a sec."

"Let us gather our things," Miles snapped his bag shut.

"Most of our things are down in the drink," Tommy twirled the hubcap on one finger.

"Here is your coat, Miles," Dale held up his suit jacket while she looked down at the ground.

Miles took his jacket and drew her close, "I can take you home, Dale. We don't have to go on tonight. Would you like to…"

"No," she smiled a slight coquettish smile, "I'll be fine, but thank you for the offer."

Somewhere up above them, the sound of the rope in the grass thumped.

"Here ya' are!"

"This way!" Tommy started to toss the hubcap away, but tucked it under his arm instead and started up the steep incline.

Miles placed his jacket over Dale's shoulders and drew her close. She pulled the lapels together and leaned into him. He put his arm around her and led her up the hill.

When they reached the top, the farmer took their hands and pulled them up to the road. He had an old wooden wagon mostly filled with loose hay and pulled by two large dark horses. The farmer himself was dressed in overhauls and a straw hat. He tipped the hat to Dale.

"Ma'am."

"Thank you," Dale replied.

"Nice hat," Miles said as he climbed up into the back of the wagon.

"Eh, er.. Thank ya' kindly," the farmer tipped his hat to Miles.

"No, I mean… nice hat," Miles looked down on him and repeated, "Those overalls new?"

Tommy sat on the edge of the wagon. He looked over into Miles' dark eyes.

"Well, I…" the farmer looked down at his outfit, "The missus, she bought 'em fer mah birthday last week… uh…"

Miles looked away as the farmer's voice trailed off. He set his coat and bag and Dale's purse in a wooden side box that held some tools.

"Well, let's get you into…" the farmer climbed up the front of the wagon and took the reins. With a slight pull, the wagon started moving along the road.

The trio sat in silence for a few moments, gently swaying to the rocking wagon. They let their legs dangle off the back. Dale put her head on Miles' shoulder and closed her eyes.

"I guess we don't…" Tommy held the hubcap out to toss it aside.

"Keep it," Miles voice was getting as dark as the growing darkness of the night that he was staring into.

"What do we need a…"

Miles looked back over his shoulder to a pitchfork lying at the edge of the hay. "Let me ask you a question, Tommy," he said.

"Oh, no," Dale sat up and looked into Miles' face, "not the question."

"It's just a question, Dale," Tommy set the hubcap on his lap and tightened his bow tie, "I always like the question."

"It's not just the question that bothers me," Dale looked around, "It's the thing that always follows the question. That look on your face means we're going into battle."

"Here's the question," Miles licked his lips. He reached back behind him and put his hand on the handle of the pitchfork. "If you were a farmer," he said, "Let us say you were going under cover as a farmer. What would you wear?"

"I'm sure I'd wear a straw hat," Tommy smiled.

"Yes? A new one?"

"No, but it's not out of the ordinary, necessarily," Tommy said, "and overhauls too."

"That's part of the uniform, I suppose," Miles drew the pitchfork ever closer.

"Everyone knows that."

"Yes, of course," Miles said, "Tell me… What footwear would you choose?"

"Footwear? You mean like boots?" Tommy shrugged, "or maybe leather work boots?"

"You mean… you wouldn't wear Oxford wing tips?"

"For slopping out pig pens?" Tommy grimaced.

"Now let me ask a question," Dale's eyes grew wide, "Since when does hay smell like aftershave?"

"And wouldn't you send somebody back to check on the job if you ran someone off the road over a cliff?" Miles added.

All three of them slowly turned their head to look at the driver. As if on cue, he slapped the reins, and the horses took off. The trio nearly fell out of the back of the wagon as it bumped along the narrow road. Three men in suits rose up out of the hay. One of them held a gun.

"Holy cats!" Tommy stood and held the hubcap up to his chest.

Miles stood with Dale behind him.

"Finish the job!" the middle man reached into his coat.

As the wagon hit a small pothole, they all swerved to one side. Miles stomped the head of the curved pitchfork and the tool's handle flew up into his hand. The man on the left aimed to shoot Miles, but was distracted as Tommy rushed him. The man fired as Miles smacked the gun away with the tines of the tool and blocked the other two men with the handle. The bullet shot through the edge of the hubcap in Tommy's hand, and deflected off.

"That's handy," Tommy said as he smacked the man in the face with the hubcap, "Maybe I oughta' bring this on all our cases.

The man staggered back as Tommy smacked the gun out of his hand with the chrome disc.

Miles bopped the man on the right in the nose with the end of the handle. The man fell back in the loose hay. A stream of blood flew from his nose.

"Looks like I found another use for a pitchfork, too," Miles dropped the tool and grabbed the gun that the middle man pulled from his jacket.

The man landed a blow to Miles' jaw with his left hand. Miles shrugged it off and pulled the gun away. "Who do you work for?" Miles demanded.

The man on the left jumped up and at Tommy, but he slipped on the hay and fell short. Tommy reacted by slinging the hub cap like a discus, only missing when the man fell. The hub cap smacked into the back of the head of the driver and knocked him unconscious and off the wagon onto the road.

"Or maybe not," Tommy said.

The man on the right crawled down the wagon, holding his bloody nose. Miles lifted the middle man up by the lapels. "Who?" Miles' voice was taking on a darker complexion.

Tommy jumped towards the driver's seat, but was intercepted by the man on the left who grabbed his foot and caused him to fall.

"Ak!"

The middle man brought up his knee and kicked back from Mile's grasp. They began exchanging blows as Tommy and the left man rolled around in the hay punching and choking each other. Everyone who was standing fell to the floor as the horses ran wild around a sharp turn. They all balled together on one side of the wagon, kicking and choking and punching en masse.

"Alley OOP!" Tommy kicked one man up over the edge.

"Aaaakkk!" The man hit the ground and rolled into the bushes along the road like a sack of beat up potatoes.

"Who?" Miles pounded the face of the middle man.

"Tommy smacked the man in the face..."

"Say goodbye, cowboy," Tommy tossed the man over the edge.

"No!" Miles reached out and grabbed the man by the wrist as he flew by.

"I thought…" Tommy slipped around on the hay.

Miles held tight to the man as they flew down the bumpy road. The man's heels scraped mercilessly on the ground. His shoes flew off into the weeds.

"AAAHH!" the man screamed.

"Who do you work for!?" Miles leaned over the edge, his long black hair down in his face, waving in the wind.

The man reached into his vest and pulled out a knife. Miles let go and dropped the man along the road. Dale screamed. It seemed like a good time to do so.

"Dale!"

The last man was holding Dale in front of him. He had his arm around her and a knife to her head. He stood on the wood near the back of the wagon. Blood ran from his nose down his face.

"Stop this wagon," he said, "or the girl gets it."

"Tommy?" Miles planted his feet in the middle of the wagon.

"On it, Doc," Tommy scrambled to get to the driver's seat.

Tommy made his way forward and got hold of the loose reins. The man walked up towards the middle of the wagon, keeping his eyes on Miles and the knife on Dale. As he passed Miles, Miles stomped on the end of the pitchfork that was hidden in the hay. The handle flew up and at the man. He instinctively guarded himself. Dale took the distraction and brought her elbow back into the man's gut. As he pulled the knife away, she reached up and put her arms around the man's neck, and in a swift practiced move, she doubled over and flung the man over her, off the wagon and into the road.

"Daaaaa!" the man screamed as he rolled over and over on the ground.

"Got control!" Tommy said, "But I ain't slowing down until I get some distance between us and them."

"Wait…" Miles put his arm out and Dale collapsed into him, "Never mind. Go!"

Miles kicked the pitchfork out of the way, and the two sat down in the hay together until Tommy finally slowed the wagon to a stop. It was very dark, but as the horses stepped forward out of the shade of a large old tree, they could see the stars and the full moon cast a light blue glow over the long rows of corn.

"There's one thing the city doesn't have," Miles said softly.

"Yeah?" Tommy walked up alongside of the wagon, "The city also don't have hay wagons full of crooks trying to kill you."

"You're forgetting the Case of the Vetted Farmer," Miles smiled.

"Okay, except for that one time."

"Well, we've really done it now," Dale pulled sprigs of hay from her hair, "I can sew up some of the rips in your slacks, but this really is a royal mess."

"Don't worry about it," Miles climbed out of the wagon and put out his hand to help Dale down.

"I'm sure I have a small sewing kit in my purse," Dale took her purse from the side box and opened it up.

"You got a deli sandwich in there?" Tommy looked over her shoulder.

"There will be food at the party," Miles put his hand on his chin in thought. He walked up to the edge of the tall corn rows. "You know," he turned back to Tommy, "I'm going to need your pants," and he slipped into the corn and disappeared.

"Did he just say he needed my pants?" Tommy stared into the corn, "Hey, Doc…"

"Huff!" Miles grunted from somewhere amidst the field. The stalks started swaying as he came back out carrying something human sized.

"What do you know," he threw the scarecrow on the ground, "a farmer's costume."

"Uh, definitely more worn that what those guys were wearing," Tommy lightly kicked the stuffing, "What's that got to do with my pants."

"I'm going to need your pants, farmer Brown," Miles said, "I have a swanky party to go to."

"I still don't…"

"You need to go undercover," Miles unbuckled his belt.

"In this old outfit?" Tommy kicked the scarecrow a little harder.

"I need you snooping around the servant's quarters and behind the scenes. Find out what they know," Miles emptied his pockets and set the contents on the wagon, "Pants please."

Tommy took off his belt, "Yeah, but…"

He looked behind him at Dale. She was smiling and watching the men. When she realized what she was doing, she stood straight and blushed.

"Ya' mind?" Tommy unzipped his drawers.

"Oh! I'm…" Dale covered her good eye and turned around.

"There ain't no boots on this thing," Tommy kicked off his pants and looked down on the scarecrow.

"Let's hope they don't notice what we noticed," Miles took the pants from Tommy, "At least you get to wear your own shoes."

"Swell," Tommy knelt down and started taking the stuffing out of the old clothes, "Hey, there's bugs in here!"

A short time later, they were arriving at the gates of the Carlisle mansion. Miles and Dale sat on either side of an itchy Tommy, who was driving the team.

"Hold on there!" a guard stopped them as they entered the driveway.

"Ah, my good man," Miles spoke up, "I'm Doctor Murdock. I was expected here tonight, albeit somewhat earlier. I had a mishap on the road. This kind local was nice enough to give us a ride."

The guard looked them up and down. Tommy hid his shoes and chewed on a sprig of hay.

"That's fine," the guard said, "Things have only really gotten started just recently anyway since Mr. Carlisle showed up."

"Howdy," Tommy tipped his hat and a piece of it came off in his hand.

"I promised the good man he could feed his horses in exchange for picking us up," Miles handed the guard his identification, "I hope that's not too much trouble."

"I suppose..." the guard handed the wallet back, "Stable's around back. Take care of your business and leave. This is a private party. Drop the doctor and his date off at the front door."

"So much for snacks," Tommy mumbled.

"I'd volunteer to stash some away for you, but I don't know as I'll have the pocket space," Miles patted his coat.

"You don't suppose the Purple Scar will make an appearance?" Tommy said.

"Well, that depends," Miles looked around.

"Depends on what?"

"On which Purple Scar you are talking about," Miles grew dark, "Remember why we're here. This is more of a mission for Miles Murdock than the Purple Scar."

"Yeah, that's not what I picked up," Tommy nodded, "You acted all broody when I brought in that paper."

"Do you think this makeup will disguise my bump? Dale applied copious powder to her face.

"It will be fine," the Purple Scar spoke from Miles' mouth, "The disguise will hide all the injury."

Dale and Tommy turned to him. Tommy stopped the wagon.

"Miles?"

"I'm… I'm fine," Miles rubbed his forehead, "I just can't stomach some crook usurping my alter ego for his own ends. It makes me a little… edgy. I know why we're here. I remember why we're here."

"Hands in the air, 'Purple Scar'!" Detective Griffin pointed the gun and the flashlight at the back of the dark disfigured figure holding a barely conscious crook in his hands.

The alley way stank of the lesser parts of Akelton City, the parts where the detective and the vigilante often came across one another. Even at two a.m., the stench of evil prevailed on the nostrils. Sometimes, that's when it was its strongest.

"Griffin," the Purple Scar snarled, small droplets of fleshy liquid fell on the criminal's dazed face, "What is the meaning of this?"

"We had a deal," Griffin walked ever closer.

"We have no deals."

"We had an understanding, then," Griffin stood tall, shoulders back, "Killing crosses the line."

"I haven't…" Purple Scar looked down at the man in his grip. He threw him down on the ground at Detective Griffin's feet, "Not in front of the children."

"Who are you?" Griffin ordered, "What's going on here?"

The man started to stand. Griffin put his boot on his back and forced him flat to the wet cobblestones.

"Get me away from that thing!" the man begged, "I know three guys he's offed in as many nights!"

"I've been looking for you, Benny Kirkster, AKA, Benny the Slimeball," Griffin pushed down harder on the man.

"Whatever, just…" Benny wiped the slime from his face, "Just get me away from him!"

"Tell me your name, and we can settle this," Griffin demanded to the Scar.

"I told you…" Purple Scar fell into the shadows and vanished, "Not here!"

Griffin lowered his gun. He lifted the crook up by the back of his jacket and pushed him back towards the street. As he got into the light, his partner jumped up out of the car and handcuffed Benny.

"Did you see him?" the young stocky man opened the back door and shoved Benny in, "Did you see the Purple Scar?"

"I don't want to talk about it now, Jiminy," Griffin pinched the bridge of his nose.

"Uncle Daaan," Jiminy pulled up close and whispered, "Not in front of the bad guys, remember?"

"Oh, right, uh, James," Griffin walked around the front passenger side of the car, "I mean, Officer Griffin."

After only a few seconds in the car, Jiminy was looking out the windows, "He's out there, I know."

"Look, Jimin.. James, we're heading up to Swank Street to visit a doctor friend of mine. I need his help on something."

"Jeepers, sir," Jiminy gripped the wheel, "It's two-thirty in the morning."

"He'll be up," Griffin said, "At least, I sure hope he'll be up. He'd better be up."

"Shouldn't we drop this guy off at the precinct first?" Jiminy pointed his thumb back to the back seat.

"What? Oh, yeah, I guess so," Griffin said, "Head back there first. I need a strong cup of Joe anyway."

After the men left the precinct headquarters, they drove up to Doctor Murdock's mansion. The lights on the second floor were lit. There was a wide curved staircase leading up to the resident quarters. They parked out front and walked up the staircase. As Griffin prepared to knock, Miles opened the door with flourish.

"Dan, what the devil was all that business…?" Miles frowned.

"Uh, Doctor Murdock, I'd like you to meet my nephew Jiminy," Griffin opened his hand towards Jiminy.

"Sorry to bother you so early, doctor," Jiminy gave a slight bow and wiped his boots.

"Detective Griffin!" Miles smiled widely and stepped back, "What brings you out so late tonight? Please… come on in."

As the men walked through the doorway, Jiminy hissed between his teeth, "Captain remember!"

"Oh my, of course," Griffin shook his head, "I keep forgetting. Doctor Murdock, this is James Griffin, Officer James Griffin. He's new."

"I'm not the same kid you remember from grade school, sir," Jiminy said.

"Yes, yes," Griffin said.

"How do you… do?" Miles shook his hand absentmindedly, but then paused and stared at his face.

"Fine... I'm sure?" Jiminy pulled his hand out of Miles' hand.

"What could bring you here tonight, Captain?" Miles tightened the belt on his long purple robe, "that we need to discuss so urgently?"

"Yes, I know what you mean," Griffin put his hands behind his back, "Well, there is one thing."

"Do tell," Miles poured a glass of bourbon, "Mind if I have a drink?"

"Jeepers," Jiminy looked around in awe. The walls were filled with hunting trophies and masks and certificates of accomplishment, "You a hunter, Mr. Murdock?"

"You could say that," Miles took a sip and leaned back on the counter, "Although nowadays I'm more of a specialist."

"Actually, I'm here on business from the Mayor," Griffin raised his finger, "Yes, Mayor Crenshaw wanted me to speak with you about your talents... your doctor talents, specifically as it has to do with plastic surgery."

"Really?" both Miles and Jiminy turned towards him in surprise.

"Uh, yes," Griffin looked back and forth at the two men, "Yes, of course."

Miles set down his drink.

"Mayor Crenshaw wants you to look into possible criminal activities of Fletcher Carlisle," Griffin said, "He's suspected of extortion, money laundering, underground criminal activity, impersonation and a host of other infractions including murder. This is all hush, hush, you know, strictly between us."

"You sure he's not just trying to get some dirt on his rival for the mayoral election coming up?" Miles offered Griffin a cigarette, "Throw something up against the wall to see what sticks?"

"It's not for me to say," Griffin held up his hand, "There's a mountain of circumstantial evidence leading to possible corruption, but pick any millionaire nowadays, and who can't come up with something they're hiding."

"Mm," Miles lit himself a smoke, then he handed the pack to Jiminy, "You smoke, son?"

"He doesn't smoke, Miles," Griffin interrupted, "What do you think?"

"You, uh, you like the fights, kid?" Miles put the cigarettes in his robe pocket, "You look like you might have seen a few boxing matches."

Jiminy stood and stared straight into Miles' eyes. He frowned and clenched his jaw.

"I don't have to tell you anything," Jiminy said through clenched teeth.

"What the...?" Griffin stepped in between them, "Go to the car, James."

"Captain!"

"Do what I say, boy!" Griffin barked at Jiminy.

Jiminy sneered and ran out of the room, slamming the door behind him.

"Just what was the meaning of all this, then?" Griffin got up in Miles' face, "And what is with this new Purple Scar scare I've been seeing? Are we shooting the suspects now?"

"I have nothing to do with it," Miles placed his bottle back on the shelf and poured his drink down the small bar sink. He took a long drag on his cigarette and crushed it in a gold ashtray, "All I know is what I've read in the newspapers."

"So you haven't started using a calling card?" Griffin rifled through his pockets.

"What are you talking about?"

Griffin pulled out a business card with a large jagged purple scar on one side. He tossed it on the bar.

"I've never seen this before," Griffin looked the card over, "Where did you get it?"

"Salvatore Ritchie," Griffin took the card from Miles' hand, "What was left of him, anyhow."

"I've put Ritchie down a dozen times, Dan. Why would I kill him?"

"Why haven't you stopped him?"

"Ritchie?"

"You know who." Griffin stuffed the card back in his pocket.

"I haven't been able to find him yet," Miles said, "The regulars are too spooked to talk. I didn't realize it could work to my disadvantage to have them too scared."

"Yeah? Well, us cops aren't all useless," Griffin said, "Metronelli gave up a lead."

"How did you get him to talk?" Miles sat down in an antique wicker chair with a huge woven back, "Have a seat."

Griffin sat on the corner of a chrome table, "Dead men'll often give you the answers you need."

"Dead men?"

"We found him minutes before he died," Griffin looked down, "He was plugged full of holes. He bled out before we even got him to the hospital."

"You know who this fake Scar is?"

"Nope," Griffin said, "but we know who he works for, who Metronelli says, anyway."

"Who?" Miles leaned forward.

"You'll never guess."

"No."

"Coincidence?"

"Carlisle?" Miles stood.

"I take it you'll look into this for us?" Griffin watched as Miles strolled to the window and looked out into the night, "Heard he's having a big bash tomorrow. Bet we can get a well off donor like you a couple of tickets."

"I need to get some sleep, Captain," Miles closed the drapes. "This political intrigue doesn't really sound like something I should get involved in."

"I can have the invitations here by lunch."

"That sounds fine," Miles walked away, lost in thought. He walked into the next room.

"You want I should see myself out?" Griffin stood.

After a moment of silence, Griffin walked to the door. He placed his hand on the knob.

"Oh, Captain," Miles reentered the room, "has young Jiminy been in an accident?"

"How do you know about that?"

"It's just…" Miles ran his fingers across his ear. "A good plastic surgeon can recognize another surgeon's work, sometimes even down to signature tucks and cuts."

"See why the mayor wanted you to check out Carlisle," Griffin pointed. "You'll be able to tell if he's had work done, if he's hiding something. Maybe he's not even who he says he is."

"I doubt that very much," Miles rubbed his chin in thought, "That drastic of surgery is for the dime novels, not real life. I was just concerned about the signature moves I saw on Jiminy. They were probably nothing…"

"Look, Doc," Griffin stepped closer to Miles. "You got to understand. Jiminy was making a name for himself in the local boxing circuit. He fell in with the wrong crowd, is all. They messed him up pretty bad. Somehow, my sister found him the medical help he needed, but he had to do some shady boxing to pay off his debts."

"I'm familiar with the practice."

"After a year or so, he rabbited, ran here to Akelton," Griffin waved his hand, "He wanted a fresh start, wanted to be a cop like his uncle. I kind of took him under my wing, pulled a few strings."

"I'm sure that's it," Miles said. "Give him my apologies. Tell him I was

"He fell in with the wrong crowd…"

drunk or something."

"He puts on a good face, but underneath, there's still a lot of scars," Griffin opened the door.

"I understand."

"I'll be here in the morning bright and early at eight o'clock with the invites," Griffin stepped out into the night.

"You'll be here at noon," Miles partially closed the door.

"Right."

"I'll be gone."

"Of course."

Miles closed the door. Griffin sighed and put his hands in his pockets. He turned and nearly walked into Jiminy who was standing in the bushes.

"What did he say?" Jiminy stood in the shadows.

"Oh, he'll... he'll give it some thought," Griffin walked past Jiminy towards the car, "Let's go."

"He's going to the party, isn't he," Jiminy stepped down the steps.

"How did you...?"

"I heard you talking with Mayor Crenshaw on the phone about getting Doctor Murdock to the party to check on Carlisle," Jiminy said.

"I'm sure he'll come through for us," Griffin opened the car door, "He always does."

+++

"You there! Who are you?"

Tommy spun around in the moonlit stable yard.

"Oh, uh... Hunter... Pheasant... Pheasant Hunter!" Tommy sputtered, "I... uh..."

"Your name is Pheasant Hunter?" The man in the blue suit and floppy hat jogged up to Tommy, "What kind of..."

"Hunter Pheasant," Tommy stuck out his hand, "My parents were... funny."

"Well you ain't with the party, that's for sure," the man shook Tommy's hand and looked him up and down, "Anyway, you ain't supposed to be out back here. Deliveries go to the side door."

"No, no, I just got hired," Tommy looked around, "I was told to report to the guy in charge of... all this back here."

"The boss said he was taking on a few extra hands to watch the place tonight," the man scratched the back of his head, "I suppose you could..."

"Yes, the boss told me that, too," Tommy scratched the back of his head, "He said he needed some extra hands, an extra set of eyes is what he said, to help with the watching of the place tonight... because of the party."

"There's about a half dozen of us spread around the yard," the man pointed into the darkness, "Plus my kids are wandering around here somewhere. Probably getting into trouble. I swear, if their mother..."

"I'll just meander, then," Tommy took a few steps, "you know, look around."

"Carter didn't assign you a post?"

"Carter?" Tommy paused, "Oh, Carter! Well, I haven't exactly..."

"He's over by the box," the man pointed his thumb back over his shoulder and winked, "of course. He never lets anybody else take that post."

"Well, of course he doesn't," Tommy started walking in the direction the man was pointing, "That would be... silly. No one would expect anybody but Carter to guard the... box, because, you know, the box... is... over there?"

"Yeah, of course..." the man squinted and tilted his head, "Say... how come you..."

"I'll head on over there, then," Tommy picked up his pace, "I'll talk to Carter at the box."

Tommy rounded the corner and looked down the side of a long storage shed filled with tractors and implements. The front of the building had been built open with no doors, and he could just make out a small room built on at the end. There was a dim bulb sticking out of the wall next to the door, and a man sat on the step, smoking a cigarette. Tommy took off his ragged straw hat and tossed it onto the metal seat of an old planter. He went to tighten his bow tie, but realized he wasn't wearing it anymore. Instead, he rubbed the back of his neck and took a deep breath and started walking towards Carter. As he approached, Carter looked up from a battered magazine and flicked his cigarette at him.

"Go away, pal," he said through his smoke, "You don't wanna be here."

"No, I just..." Tommy kept walking, but looked around and behind him, "You're Carter?"

"What of it?"

"The boss told me to report to you."

"The boss?" Carter stood a long way up. He was a foot taller than Tommy, but rail thin in his Zoot suit. He tossed the magazine on the ground.

"Yeah, you know..." Tommy followed Carter all the way up, "the boss."

Tommy stuck his hand out. Carter ignored it. Tommy stuck his hands in his pockets.

"What's your story?" Carter sneered.

"I'm, uh, Pheasant," Tommy rolled his eyes, "Hunter Pheasant."

"Pheasant?" Carter cocked his head, "Your name's Pheasant?"

"Well, you see…"

"You any kin of the Carolina Pheasants?" Carter pulled a toothpick out of his vest pocket, "I grew up with a gal from Carolina named Pheasant."

"Oh, the Carolina Pheasants," Tommy smiled, "Yes, of course. We're, ah, distant cousins. What's her name?"

"Carolina."

"That's…" Tommy looked at the old door behind Carter. He sidestepped Carter and placed his hand on the black glass knob, "Say, what's in here?"

Carter clamped down on Tommy's wrist. He pulled a knife from his vest and held it in front of Tommy's face. "How bad you wanna know, hayseed?"

Tommy stepped back and pulled his hand away. He backed up another step, rubbing his wrist.

"You're awfully curious for hired muscle," Carter took a step towards Tommy, "Maybe you should just stick to your own business and let me do mine."

"Well, technically, if I was guarding something," Tommy put his hand up and leaned against a support post in a casual manner, "I would want to know what I was guarding."

"You just look out for any funny business," Carter said, "You know, like strangers nosing around asking too many questions."

"Ah, like that. Gotcha," Tommy fumbled with an old horseshoe hanging from a nail. He took a step closer to the post.

"Why don't you take yourself over to the…" Carter turned his head and pointed his knife towards the back of the house.

Tommy pulled the horseshoe down and swung around in a circle, catching Carter in the chin with the metal object.

"CHUH!" Carter spun around, spitting out a tooth. He landed beside an old harrow and laid there in the dirt unconscious.

"I certainly hope this is worth it," Tommy unlatched the clasps on his overall bib and stepped up next to Carter. He slipped out of the dirty clothes and propped Carter's unconscious body up on the implement. He pulled Carter's jacket and pants off and climbed into them. He cuffed up the pants and slipped the large hat on.

"Never really got the whole Zoot suit scene," he said to himself, "Hepcat."

He found a key in the pocket and fit it into the lock. It worked. The door opened, but it was too dark to see what exactly was inside. As Tommy stepped up to get a closer look, he heard someone running up behind him. Tommy spun around and down, grabbing Carter's knife from the ground. "Hey, mister!" a boy about nine years old ran up to him. Another, somewhat younger boy soon followed. They were dressed in rags and were as dirty as the night, "What's goin' on?"

"You kids run along!" Tommy ordered, "I'm just... You kids run along now."

"Is that Mister Carter?" the boy pointed to Carter sprawled out on the harrow.

"He's in his underwear!" the younger boy covered his mouth and snorted.

"You said, underwear," the first boy laughed along.

"He's bleeding," the younger boy stopped laughing and looked up into Tommy's face.

They both got quiet. Their eyes grew large and they backed up a step. The older boy stepped in front of the younger boy. "Go get Pops," he whispered.

"Eeeee!" the little boy screamed in a pitch that sounded like a barn owl in a dive.

"No no no!" Tommy stepped towards them, but they took off in a dead run.

He ran after them, but they were adept at skittering away. He stopped at the edge of the long shed.

"Doggone it!" he turned around, "I'd better make quick work of this."

"Hey, you!" a voice called out, "Pheasant Hunter!"

Tommy turned to the voice of the man he had met earlier, "That's, Hunter Pheas..."

Tommy darted to the door and took the knob. He swung the old door back, but was stopped when the man grabbed him off the step by the back of his jacket and threw him on the ground.

"No you don't!" the man slammed the door closed and started stepping ever closer, "What in tarnation are you doing here? What did you do to Carter? Why are you wearing his clothes?"

Tommy grabbed the horseshoe out of the dirt. The man kicked it from his hand.

"Answer me!" the man ordered, "You were in such a hurry to yak away before."

"Sure, but then I was trying to gain your confidence," Tommy crab walked backwards.

The man tried to stomp on Tommy, but Tommy rolled over and up in a single move. He raised his fists and danced back and forth from foot to foot.

"You want some of what Carter got?"

"Get 'im, Pops!" one of the boys shouted from the roof of the shed.

Tommy looked up and was cold cocked by Pops' left fist.

"Oof!" Tommy fell back against a tractor. His hat flew back onto the ground. Pops moved in on him. Tommy leaned back on the large metal wheel and kicked both feet into the man's chest. The man stumbled backwards out into the moonlight and landed on a bucket.

"Raa!" Pops threw the bucket into the shed at Tommy, but missed.

The two stumbled towards each other.

"C'mon, Dempsey," Tommy raised his fists again, "Let's see what you got."

The boys rained stones down on Tommy, but he wasn't falling for that trick again.

"Cut it out!" Tommy ducked Pops' fist.

"You don't tell my kids what to do!" Pops' next punch just glanced Tommy's ear.

Tommy threw a right, but it was blocked. Pops came up with a midsection cut with his left that knocked the wind right out of Tommy.

"Woof!" Tommy landed on his knees and caught Pops' boot with both hands as he tried to kick him. He twisted hard, knocking Pops off balance. Both men jumped back and up.

"We don't have to fight," Tommy said behind his fists.

"It's my job to fight," Pops hopped back and forth in a semi-crouched position.

"My employer would pay you a lot more to just be a gardener," Tommy took a jab, but missed. The men switched positions.

"Not a chance, Pheasant," Pops swung, but Tommy blocked.

"The name's Pedlar," Tommy backed up a step and stood straight, "Tommy Pedlar. I have a proposition for you."

"Nope!" Pops hit Tommy in the cheek beside his nose. Tommy fell back into the shed post and wiped the blood from his nose.

"Uuuuhh!" the boys flattened out on the shaking roof.

"Think of your boys!" Tommy put his hands up to shield himself, "I can get you a proper job!" He closed his eyes in anticipation.

Pops stood in front of him with his fists clenched at his side. "Talk fast, but clear, Pheasant," he said.

"I work for a rich guy," Tommy slowly took his arms down, "a doctor. He needs a gardener and a landscaper for a project he has going on behind his house. He can pay you good, and give you and your boys a place to stay."

"A doctor?" Pops looked deep into Tommy's eyes. "If we'd a had a doctor when the boys' ma got sick, she mighta' still been here."

"I know for a fact that he will treat you and them for free," Tommy looked back straight into Pops' eyes, "a fact!"

"Buddy, if you're lyin' to me…"

"I just need to see what Carter was guarding, is all," Tommy slipped away from Pops and a little closer to the door.

Carter moaned and started to move.

"I just need to tie Carter to this machine and then see what he was guarding, is all," Tommy took a roll of binder twine from a shelf and proceeded to wrap it around and around the dazed Carter.

"Waht arse muh…" Carter mumbled and pulled against the thin ropes, "skivvies!"

Pops pulled up close to Tommy and whispered, "Look, if he sees me with you…"

"Pop! Pop!" the boys came running around.

"Head to the kitchen," Tommy said, "It should be safe there."

Pops took his boys by their shoulders and herded them away. Tommy opened the door and reached inside. He stopped short, wide eyed. The breath caught in his throat for a moment.

"Holy cats," he whispered under his quivering breath, "It's… the Purple Scar…"

"Blast!" Miles dug through his black leather bag, "It's all in disarray!"

"I know, just look at me!" Dale sat at the table and frantically worked her hair from her reflection in her compact.

"I'm talking about my bag," Miles found his light and turned the bag on the table so he could see better.

"Just look at all the beautiful women here," Dale said, "Just look at them!"

"Miles looked up around the room, "Yes? So?"

"You cad!" Dale slapped her purse shut. "How dare you look at other women when you're out with me!"

"Dale, you are a true joy sometimes," Miles continued through his bag, "I was, in fact surveying the room."

"Is that so," Dale pinched her mouth. "This room is so full of people, you couldn't survey anything, especially not in the short time you looked up."

"There are armed men at each exit, two of which have criminal records." Miles pulled out a broken vial and frowned. "Several of the women here are paid escorts. Three politicians and a school board member are here with women other than their wives. There is a hidden dagger in the chandelier and a secret room behind the post next to the kitchen. Also, they are out of paper in the lavatory."

"You couldn't... How did you...? Oh!" Dale slammed her purse down on her lap, "I hate it when you do that. You're making some of that up."

"I could continue."

"Don't."

Miles pulled forth another broken vial, "Blast!"

"Let's just hope nobody needs a doctor tonight, Miles dear," Dale placed her hand on his arm.

"It's not that, Dale," Miles stood up straight and looked around, "I was... Say, that's odd."

"What is it?" Dale twisted in her chair, but could only see a sea of suits and gowns.

"It's the captain's nephew, Jiminy."

"I thought the police were staying back," Dale leaned in, "to keep people from suspecting."

"They are," Miles rubbed his chin, "He is heading towards the kitchen. Listen, Dale, I need to go check this out. You stay here."

"Oh no you don't," I'm not going to be at this table all by myself," Dale put her hand up to her face to shield her mouth, "everyone staring at my ruined outfit and my monstrous eye and my wind blown hair."

"I need you to watch for an opening to get to Carlisle's table," Miles brought another vial out of his bag. "We may never get another opening all night if we don't take advantage of the first one we find."

"I'm having a perfectly miserable night," Dale put her hands on her hips, "The least you could do is have one with me."

"Drink sir?" a waiter stopped at their table, "Madame?"

"I don't touch the stuff," Miles waved. "Not that cheap swill."

"I'll take one," Dale reached out. "I may need something to throw in somebody's face if he doesn't straighten out."

"Very good, ma'am," the waiter handed her the drink and walked off, weaving his way through the crowd.

"I thought Miles Murdock was a lush," Dale took a sip. "You have an identity to maintain."

"Yes perhaps," Miles said. "I'm just upset at the state of my bag, is all. I had such a plan. Now I can't even get close enough to check out Carlisle. Fine, let us retire to the kitchen to follow up on young Jiminy Griffin. Keep in mind, if there's trouble…"

"Yes, I know," Dale sipped her drink. "Stay out of the way. What about all those self defense lessons you've been giving me. I did all right with that thug on the wagon, didn't I? Was all that just an excuse to wrap your arms around me?"

Miles stood with his bag and presented his arm, "Milady, care to jostle the upper class snobbery with me?"

"Certainly, I'm sure," Dale stood and took his arm.

They weaved and tripped their way through the standing throng, apologizing and holding each other up.

"He may have gone into the secret passageway," Miles pointed towards the kitchen.

"I don't see…"

"Behind that large portrait is a trip switch that unlocks the sliding door," Miles said. "The pillar keeps people away and hides the fact that someone has used the door."

"Hey, that's like the one…"

"I have at home, yes," Miles gave her arm a squeeze. "Plus, the mayor gave Captain Griffin a copy of the blueprints to bring over with the invitations."

"You cheat sometimes," Dale smiled and squeezed back. "Don't you."

"Hold on," Miles turned them ninety degrees. "Change in plan. There is an opening at Carlisle's table."

"Can we get there in time?" Dale trotted double time in tiny bunny steps.

"Pardon me. Excuse me. Pardon… Pardon me," Miles gently pushed his way through, dragging Dale behind him.

"Murdock!" Carlisle's jaw dropped and he jumped to his feet as they arrived and pushed Mr. and Mrs. Appelton III out of the way.

"Carlisle!" Miles set his bag on the floor under the chairs and stuck out his hand across the table. "Surprised to see us?"

"Humph! Well, I... That is... Of course, I..." Carlisle stammered.

"Oh you men!" Dale waved her hand once and looked around.

"You know Nurse Dale Jordon, I assume?" Miles said. "She was with me on the ride over here."

"Miss Jordan," Carlisle gave a slight bow.

"Charmed, I'm sure," Dale gave a hint of a curtsy. "You two catch up. If you'll excuse me, I need to powder my nose."

"Now's not the time, Dale," Miles said out of the corner of his mouth.

"Just going to the little girl's room, dear," Dale slipped into the mass and vanished.

"Dale, wait," Dale heard somewhere behind her, followed by, "Blasted woman."

As she approached the portrait of some foreign general on a glorious battlefield, she looked around. There were all kinds of people looking her direction, but nobody seemed to be looking at her. Nobody seemed to be looking at anybody, really. They all were like glassy eyed fish swimming in a cramped bowl. She ran her fingers down the side of the painting like she did at Miles' place behind his landscape of the Savanna, and just in the same place, it clicked open and allowed her through a narrow passage behind.

"Well, I'll be," she said to herself. "Miles is going to have to make some changes. His one of a kind hideout isn't so one of a kind."

"Miss?" Jiminy called out and startled Dale.

He was sitting with in a lightweight wooden chair next to a large desk in a very narrow room. There was a palm plant next to the desk and the wall on one side and on the other side there was just enough room to get around. No one sat behind the desk. He had his hands on his knees and he was dressed in civilian clothes.

"Are you the secretary?"

Dale looked around. "Yes, ah," she said. "That's what I am. I'm the secretary."

"Well, I got some news for Carlisle," Jiminy squirmed uncomfortably in the creaky chair.

"Please..." Dale scooted behind the desk and pulled out a pencil and pad from the top drawer, "Continue."

"He said to meet him here..."

"Mr. Carlisle..."

"Yeah," Jiminy pulled at his collar. "But I got more news for him."

"More news..."

"Yeah," he continued. "That doc got run off the road, but he survived."

Dale placed her pencil down and stared straight ahead.

"You can go ahead and write that down," Jiminy pointed, "unless you think you can just remember it."

"I'll, uh," Dale pretended to write.

"Tony and a few of the other guys are going to make sure the job gets done." Jiminy said. "Okay. Does that make us square?"

"Square?"

"Ask him if that makes us square," Jiminy pointed. "Tell him that makes us square. He gets no more info from me, and neither does Doc Hoffelmeyer. Write that down."

"A-hem!" a female voice spoke up from the other side of the room.

A tall thin woman in plain black business clothes stood by the door. She had pointy black glasses and held a clipboard across her chest. Her other hand was on her hip, and she tapped her pointy black shoe on the floor. She had a pointy black pen tucked behind her ear under her pulled back straight black hair. Jiminy looked up at her in confusion.

"I'm so glad you're here," Dale smiled and said in as polite a tone as she could muster. She stepped back from behind the desk and approached the woman. "This gentleman is..."

In a flurry of motion, Dale slapped the lady in the shoulder with her writing pad and slipped out the door.

"Hey!" Jiminy jumped up and pushed the lady in black against the wall as he rushed past her.

Dale raced out from behind the picture and made a sharp turn into the kitchen. Her dress caught on the door, though and only came loose when Jiminy barged through. The kitchen staff all pulled back in surprise as the two raced through the cooking area towards the back door. Dale pulled food off the carts and tables, and threw it back behind her at Jiminy.

"Stop it!" Jiminy slipped on a lamb chop, but caught himself on the table and jumped up to a face full of creamed corn.

"Sir! Madam!" a cook pleaded as he dodged an errant stuffed quail. "Please do not fight in the kitchen!"

"Do not bring the pies out!" another cook waved his hands to a crew in a back room.

Dale snatched an empty skillet and swung it around in the air, just missing Jiminy. A man in a blue suit and a large floppy hat stepped in the back door as they approached.

"Stop her!" Jiminy spit some sort of casserole out of his mouth and yelled. "She's onto us!"

Dale stopped short between the two men. Her eyes darted back and forth between them, as she held the skillet up in front of her. Two dirty boys pushed into the kitchen behind the man in the floppy hat. They screamed in delight, and started shoving any food they could get a hold of into their mouth. They ran around in circles and jumped up and down.

"Oh!" Dale fell to one side as her left heel broke.

Jiminy snatched her arm and pulled his fist back.

"Now, hold on, mister!" Pops pushed in front of Dale and grabbed Jiminy's fist, "You don't need to go hitting a woman."

Jiminy dropped Dale and grabbed Pops' arm. "Back off! She's…"

Pops swung over Dale at Jiminy, but missed. The boys ran through the kitchen screaming in glee and chaos, stuffing bread down their pants and throwing potatoes and asparagus at each other. Dale scrambled to drop her shoes and make it through the kitchen door on her knees into the yard outside. Behind her, Pops and Jiminy were having it out amidst the protestations of the kitchen staff and the screams of delight of the children.

She jumped up, barefooted and took off through the yard. As she rounded the house into the front yard, she saw several men gathered by the cars. She called out and began running up to them. She pulled up short, though, hoping that she hadn't been seen when she realized who they were. One man pointed, and they all turned to look at her. One man in particular caught her attention, a man who was standing in the middle of the group, a man wearing an all too familiar face over his face.

"Bring her to me!" he demanded.

"Oh my heavens!" she exclaimed, "The Purple Scar!"

"Dale, wait," Miles raised his hand and looked for Dale amidst the crowd. Finally, he turned back around to Carlisle, "Blasted woman."

"Yes, people seldom do what is expected of them," Carlisle backed his chair up from the table.

"Why so nervous, Fletcher?" Miles turned his back and swiped two cocktails off a waiter's tray as he passed by. Using his slight of hand skills, he poured the contents of a small vial into one of them. "Here, have a

"You don't need to go hitting a woman."

drink," he handed Carlisle the tainted cocktail. "Let's toast to your many victories... and occasional failure."

Miles held up a drink. A few other people in the vicinity held up their drinks too. "To Fletcher!" they said.

Carlisle smiled a twitchy smile. A bead of sweat rolled down on front of his ear as he took a drink. Miles leaned in on the table and looked at Carlisle's face. Carlisle lifted his hand and twitched a couple of fingers. Two large men in black suits started making their way through the crowd towards them.

"What do you want?" Carlisle whispered.

"Do you have any dealings with a certain doctor named Adrian Hoffelmeyer?" Miles placed his hands on the table.

"Ya' need sumpin', boss?" one of the thugs approached the table behind Carlisle.

"I need a little space, boys," Carlisle said, "a little breathing room."

"Ya' want I should..." the other thug reached into his jacket.

Miles stood straight and reached into his own jacket.

"No! You idiots!" Carlisle hissed. "I just want the crowd back a few steps."

"Kay, move it on back folks," the men opened their arms and bulldozed the closest guests back into each other. "Go getcha' sumpin' ta' eat 'er drink 'er sumpin'."

"You can't prove anything," Carlisle scooted back up to the table and leaned in.

"I can testify to my clinical knowledge of another doctor's work," Miles sat down across the table from Carlisle. "I know you had some massive plastic surgery by well known criminal surgeon Adrian Hoffelmeyer, the same man convicted of trying to alter finger prints and identities of several notorious criminals."

"There's nothing illegal about that," Carlisle said.

"I know your personal crime fighter is a fake," Miles balled up his fists, "and that he is killing or trying to kill more than just petty crooks."

"Those men were scum!" Carlisle curled his upper lip.

"Scum who were never the less entitled to due process," Miles said, "scum who weren't given to you to judge, scum who just happened to be working for rival crime bosses."

"Nonsense!" Carlisle wiped down his heavily sweating face and threw the napkin down on the table, "I feel..."

"You may not think the surgery is illegal, but the voters won't like what you're hiding," Miles stared down Carlisle.

"They like my Purple Scar," Carlisle shook his head clear and smiled. "They think I'm cleaning up the streets, which is more than the police or the other Purple Scar has been able to do."

"I wouldn't be so sure of that," Miles said. "What do you think the real Purple Scar will do when he finds out?"

"Oh, I can take care of the real Purple Scar," Carlisle wiped his eyes. "Whoa, the room..."

Another thug squeezed through the throng and approached the table. "Sir! You have a phone call in your office."

"Not now!" Carlisle scolded. "I'm in the middle of a... heh, heh..." Carlisle looked at his drink and pushed it away from him on the table. "Can't you see that Mr... Doctor... Mr. Doctor and I are having an conversation?"

"Sir, I think you are gonna want to take this call," the man said.

"I can take him to his office," Miles stood and set his drink down.

"This is a private call, sir," the man placed a firm hand on Miles' chest to push him into his chair, but Miles never budged. The man looked up at him in surprise, "Please have a seat, sir. Mr. Carlisle will be back in a moment."

"You stay here, Murdock," Carlisle shook his head again to clear the cobwebs. He gripped the table and stood. He took a deep breath and glared at Miles, "You'd better be here when I get back. We have some unfinished business, you and I."

"That we do," Miles sat back down. "It needs be settled promptly."

The man tapped the biggest thug on the shoulder, "Marion, clear the way."

The larger thug led them straight through the crowd, shoving partiers in every direction as they passed through. The other thug walked up to Miles and stood directly behind him with his hands crossed at his waist. Miles tried to stand as the crowd gathered back in, but the thug placed a hammy hand on his shoulder and forced him back down into the chair. Miles raised an eyebrow and looked up at the large man.

"I need a drink," Miles said.

The thug said nothing.

"I need to go to the bathroom," Miles said.

The thug said nothing.

Miles tried to stand. The thug pushed him back down.

"Don't make me hurt you," Miles said.

The thug said nothing.

Miles started to stand again. Again, the thug reached out. Miles grabbed the large wrist and twisted. In a blur of motion, he spun around and struck the thug in the nose with his elbow. Then, he kicked his knee and sent the man down to the floor, and on his way down, Miles knuckled the thug in the windpipe.

The thug said nothing, but he rolled around on the floor, trying to catch his breath.

"Excuse me, ma'am," Miles gently pushed a woman in a long evening gown back, and picked up his chair he had been sitting in and smashed it over the thug's face.

The thug said nothing, as he was unconscious. A murmur spread throughout the crowd.

"It's okay," Miles looked up at the crowd. "I'm a doctor."

Miles picked up his bag and followed where Carlisle had headed. The crowd parted and let him go through unmolested. Light jazz piano started back up as Miles reached the winding staircase that led to the second floor balcony. Soon, the crowd patter picked back up to its previous pace as someone dragged the thug into the bathroom. No one even noticed Dale run out from behind a large portrait, and a bulky man chase her into the kitchen.

Miles nodded at a couple of men walking down the stairs as he was walking up. One of the men was a little known counterfeiter. The other was a race fixer. They gave him a quick glance and continued on their way. Only a few others were in the red velvety hallway leading to Carlisle's office, and Miles soon found himself alone outside Carlisle's door. He set his bag down and opened it. He stood back up and nodded as a large older lady with a cigarette in a holder walked past and eyed him suspiciously.

"Ma'am," he said and nodded, "I'm just…"

She walked on, barely taking notice of him.

He got down on one knee and dug through his bag, tutting to himself at the sad state of it. He pulled out his stethoscope and placed it around his neck. Standing up close to the door he put the nubs in his ears and the diaphragm against the dark hardwood door.

"Well get them down there!" Carlisle said.

"Everybody's already down there," another man said.

"Don't let them get in the cars," Carlisle sounded out of breath.

"Boss, are you…?"

"Get down there and take care of them!" Carlisle ordered. "Now! I'll have to handle this myself!"

"Get in the cars…" Miles muttered.

Footsteps stomped closer in rapid succession. Miles jumped up and grabbed his bag as the door flew open.

"You!" the man who had gotten Carlisle for the call leapt at Miles and grabbed him around the neck. They stumbled back against the banister above the crowd below.

"Take him out!" Carlisle's voice growled from inside the room as the larger thug stood in the doorway.

"You got dis?" He said.

Miles smacked the man back and hit him across the face with his bag. The man flew back onto the floor at the larger thug's feet.

"Yeah, it's under control," the man said.

"Kay," the thug slammed and locked the door.

Miles dropped his bag and presented himself in a la savate stance. The corners of his mouth were etched with sharp white lines and his muscles above his right eye twitched in a manner reminiscent of a spade. To his surprise, the man also presented himself in a similar style of battle.

"Take off your jacket?" Miles offered.

"I am fine," the man said. "You?"

"I'm going to need it soon."

"Dead men do not feel the cold."

"Nice line," Miles and the man circled each other. "Mind if I use it some time?"

"You are no doctor," the man said.

"And you are no common thug," Miles replied."Xiong Pi Kim? I recognize the technique."

"I learned from a close student of his," the man said. "I am but a servant… for now."

The men dove into one another, neither one of them striking a single blow against the other. They blocked crushing moves with their deadly dance. Their feet and hands all moved independently, almost without thought, through muscle memory. They each stepped back from having barely touched one another. They panted from the mental effort if nothing else.

"Did you study his teachings?" Miles lowered his hands.

"It was mandatory before we could even learn the battle techniques."

Miles walked over and picked up his bag. "I am leaving," he said. "You will not attack a man who has resigned and no longer threatens you or your charge."

"That does not mean you may pass." The man remained on guard.

Miles walked away from the man and the door and the stairway. He turned his back on the man. As he passed by a large window, he looked down to the front yard. There, he saw a gathering of men by the cars. The man in the middle had a hold of Dale's arm. She was holding a large skillet. The man was dressed in a Zoot suit and had on the mask of the Purple Scar.

Miles dropped his bag and spun around to the window. As he did, a crash came from Carlisle's office. Carlisle smashed out of his window onto the roof below. He jumped up into the air with two pistols over his head. He was laughing maniacally and firing into the air. The people below were scattering as he landed on the lawn. Over his head was the unmistakeable mask of the Purple Scar.

Miles pulled his jacket off, turning it inside out as he did. The dark purple lining clashed terribly with the color that had previously been exposed. He slipped it back on and reached into a large secret pocket in the coat. He paused only briefly to look down the hall at the unnamed man in the fighting stance. The man stood and bowed and turned around.

"Good Lord," Miles said, "two Purple Scars!"

Miles pulled out the death mask of his beloved brother and placed it over his head.

"Let us make it three!" the Purple Scar said.

Sirens could be heard approaching the Carlisle mansion, but those gathered in the front yard had more pressing concerns. Except for a dead man in a light gray suit, the other people were all huddled behind various cars in the driveway. The Carlisle Purple Scar was staggering around, occasionally firing wildly.

"Come on out!" he shouted. "I know you're here. I saw you!"

"He's talking to you!" Dale was ducked down behind a car with the Zoot suit Scar. She held her skillet up between the two.

The Zoot suit Scar raised up just enough to look through the window of the car. Dale raised the skillet to smack him in the head, when Carlisle fired again, smashing the side window out above them. The bullet bounced off the skillet and into the bushes as Zoot suit fell to the ground.

"It's me, Dale!" he shouted up from the ground and pulled his mask halfway off, "It's Tommy! I found this outfit out back."

"I… I knew that…" Dale lowered the cast iron skillet.

"Hey, yer a fake!" a man crawled over from another car.

"Klang!!" Dale smacked him in the head with the skillet.

The crowd started pouring out of the house at the sound of the sirens. When they saw the body on the lawn, many froze. Some tried to get back in, and some headed off around the side into the woods. The screaming started when Carlisle began firing indiscriminately at them. That's when he was tackled from behind by the real Purple Scar.

He knocked the gun from Carlisle's hand and started beating him in the face. Carlisle barely seemed to notice and kicked the Purple Scar off of him.

"It's the real Purple Scar!" One of the men from behind the cars jumped up. "Get him!"

"Hope you know how to use that thing," Tommy pointed at the skillet and threw his mask on the ground. He jumped up and tackled the man who was going after the Purple Scar.

"What have you taken, man?" the Purple Scar punched Carlisle in the neck, but got no response.

"I've been waiting for you, Scar!" Carlisle slurred. "I am more powerful than you will ever be."

Carlisle set upon the Purple Scar with unbelievable speed. He knocked the wind out of him and double fisted him in the face before the Scar could even respond. The Scar kicked him back and held his face.

"Ha-ha-haaa!" Carlisle laughed. "Hoffelmeyer told me he could make me strong. He told me I could beat you, no matter what kind of creature you are."

"You cannot beat death!" the Purple Scar landed multiple blows to Carlisle, but he still stood.

"Scar!" Dale screamed as a man grabbed her from behind.

She swung the skillet back over her shoulder to try to smack him in the face, but he had too tight a grip on her. Tommy was fighting off the other two men and left himself open for a sock to the jaw when he tried to help. The man grabbed the skillet from her hand and shoved her back onto the car. He came up over her with the skillet and stopped. The Purple Scar had a hold of the skillet and was not letting go. He kicked the man behind the knees in a low sweep that knocked him to the ground. He jerked the skillet away and handed it to Dale as he was again besieged by Carlisle. The man sat up in time to see Dale standing over him, legs straddling him, skillet in both hands above her head.

"Klang!!"

"Carlisle, you mixed too many drugs!" the Purple Scar struggled to talk as he was being strangled from behind. "Whatever you... took was mixed..."

"Shut up!" Carlisle threw the Scar to the ground. He reached down to grab him again, but the Scar kicked him in the gut.

"Use this!" Dale ran up to him and handed him the skillet, "You can... Oh!"

Carlisle smacked Dale in the face and sent her across the yard unconscious.

"You..." the Purple Scar grasped the skillet handle. "Will..." he blocked a punch with the iron. "Stop!" he smacked Carlisle across the face.

Carlisle ran at him.

"Klang!!" the Scar hit him over the head.

Carlisle backed up a couple of steps and charged again.

"Klang!!" the Purple Scar responded.

Carlisle fell to one knee, but lifted his hands as claws.

"Klang!!" the Purple Scar bashed him in the face.

Carlisle fell back on his back and tried to sit up. The Purple Scar pulled out his .38 revolver from his jacket. He had taken it from his bag at the last minute, but had hoped to not use it.

"Scar!" Tommy yelled from over at the cars. He held a defeated thug by the lapels, "Hey!"

"You're..." Carlisle's head swam. The world was undulating at him. "My God... what are you?"

The Purple Scar's face bled and peeled. Demons came out of his mouth and crawled along his body. Fire shot from his eyes and smoke rose from the deep gashes in his flesh. He held a burning pistol made from hell fire and he looked down on Carlisle in judgment.

"You will live in Hell!" the voice of Satan echoed in Carlisle's ears.

"Noooooo!" Carlisle clawed at his face and fell into deep unconsciousness.

The Purple Scar put his gun away and dropped the pan. He and Tommy ran to Dale as the crowd spilled out into the yard and the police began showing up on the scene.

"She'll be fine," Tommy looked up at the Purple Scar. "She'll just have a matching shiner. What the heck happened to Carlisle?"

"He mixed some unknown stimulant with a hallucinatory cocktail I gave him in lieu of a sedative due to my bag being crushed."

"Well, go on," Tommy looked up. "I'll take care of things here."

The Purple Scar melted into the shadows and back into the house where he found his bag exactly where he had left it, except it was in perfect order. It had been reorganized by a professional.

As the police were gathering up all the unconscious crooks and the one Carlisle shot, Captain Griffin walked up to Tommy. Tommy was sitting on the grass with Dale, who was patting her face with a handkerchief.

"I suppose this is the fake one," Griffin said.

"Yep," Tommy nodded. "See for yourself. The real Purple Scar took him out."

"We may get lucky and run down a few more criminals hiding in the bushes," Griffin said. "I suppose that's what the Purple Scar is doing right now."

"No sir," Miles came around the house, with his coat over his shoulder and carrying his bag and chewing on an unlit pipe. "He'll let your boys do their job tonight."

"Oh, Miles!" Dale jumped up and ran to his arms, sobbing.

"Here's another one," Pops wobbled over to Griffin, dragging Jiminy behind him. His two boys were helping him pull.

"Jiminy?" Griffin went for his gun. "Now, hold on there!"

"Wait, Dan!" Miles held out his hand. "Jiminy was working for Carlisle. He was the one who told him we were coming to check him out."

"What? That's preposterous!" Griffin puffed.

"It's true," Dale said. "He admitted it to me."

Griffin relaxed his grip on his gun. "Jiminy? How can this be?"

"How did you know?" Dale asked Miles.

"Besides Mayor Crenshaw and Captain Griffin, Jiminy was the only other one who knew we were coming," Miles said. "He also owed a debt to Dr. Adrian Hoffelmeyer for fixing him up after his attack."

"Hoffelmeyer!" Griffin said. "The crooked surgeon?"

"That's not a debt easily paid," Miles said, "but a mother will do anything to help her child."

"Penderton," Griffin lowered his head and called over another policeman. "Take Jimin… Take James into custody."

"Sir?"

"Just do it. I'll be over in a minute."

"I'm sorry, Dan," Miles put his hand on Griffin's shoulder.

"This'll kill his mother," Griffin frowned and walked away.

"You the doc?" Pops held out a swollen hand.

"That's, uh… I'm not sure of his name, actually," Tommy said.

"Pops," Pops said. "Pops Magee. I hear you're needing a live-in gardener?"

"I… am?" Miles looked over at Tommy.

"Yeah, um, you kind of are," Tommy smiled.

"I guess I am," Miles shook his hand again.

"Yay!" the boys screamed and ran around in circles.

"Do the children come along too?" Dale tried to smile, but her face hurt.

"Oh, sure!" Pops smiled back through swollen lips. "That's Erbert and Vaylan. They're my boys."

"How sweet," Dale looked up into Miles' face.

They all walked down the yard as the last of the police cars drove away. The cool of the night was beginning to sink into their clothes.

"Uh, Miles?" Tommy said with his hands in his pockets.

"Yes, Tommy?" Miles was examining Dale's face.

"Any idea how we're going to get home tonight?" Tommy looked into the sky.

They all stopped and looked around.

"I have a wagon and a couple of horses," Pops said.

"Yay!" the boys laughed and ran off towards the stables.

"Looks like it's gonna be a long ride home," Tommy shrugged.

"I don't mind," Miles put his arms around Dale, and she put hers around him. "I don't mind at all.

THE END

BEHIND THE SCENES

The first thing I did was fall in love with these characters. Once I did that, the story flowed easily. I wrote the first draft in three days. Some writers chafe at rules and guidelines. I often flourish in a box. Sure, there are times when I want to be free, but I can do that any old time. I knew I had a story I could tell with these characters.

The short story format lets me play around with the telling somewhat. I started after a major hunk of action had taken place. Had this been a novel, I would have most certainly showed the scene. I would have led up to it with hints and foreshadowing. I didn't have the space to do that here, and it would have muddied the story. I didn't want to introduce the Purple Scar into the story, even the fake Purple Scar until the end. I could maintain a mystery about him better if I waited. In a novel, he would have had to make several appearances before the finale. I was able to focus on the ancillary characters more. I was able to show the value of Miles' real life persona. I was able to show how the side characters related to Miles and spoke of the Purple Scar, how they were necessary to the team and how Miles felt about them. It gave greater weight to Tommy's warning near the end. The reader wasn't left wondering how Tommy could have any sway over the Purple Scar. They knew his importance.

As far as the individual characters, here is how I saw them. Miles is a good guy with multiple talents. He is always working, though. His mind is too sharp to be turned off. He has two personas to perfect, and neither one of them is really all him. He carries the weight of his murdered brother close to his chest. Something that horrible that can make you take on a separate identity would tend to write over your consciousness and take over your life. He hasn't come to terms with it yet. Tommy is a reformed con man. As such, he excels in multiple aliases. It's his thing. He can be the wide eyed sidekick and genuinely believe it, but he can also be a suave sophisticate or a bumbling farm hand if necessary. He may not be as smart and talented as Miles, but he is a Jack of all trades. Dale is the love interest, yes. She is a young but talented nurse who has had to learn quite a bit under fire. She all too often puts herself in harm's way, but she is not the typical damsel in distress. Make no mistake, there is that element to be sure. This is a pulp story set in the thirties. She is not a totally modern Millie, but she's no shrinking violet either. She has some talent in other areas and is not afraid to use it. Captain Griffin is the long-suffering but good hearted policeman who helps push the story, but I wanted to give him a little more in this one. His nephew Jiminy turns out to be more than he appears. Jiminy is more a tragic figure than someone who is genuinely bad. He could be reformed. Now, the villains in a short story pulp can be very two dimensional. I wanted a few basic thugs, but I also wanted to take what little space I had to develop some surprises. In a novel, there would be side stories and sub quests. There is not the room in a short story. That doesn't mean the villains have to be all flat or all evil. The unnamed martial artist has honor. Pops has kids. Even Carter is a lot of fun to play with. I wanted to have different ways to win the fights other than a fist or a gun. Using a horseshoe and a frying pan and a pitchfork was different and unexpected. When it came to Carlisle, I needed to make him more than just a thug. If I had the space, I would have made him an underling and continued up the chain of command. As it was, I had to settle for him being the main bad guy. He was smart and rich and successful, but he also had an ace up his sleeve, a mysterious benefactor that gave him super powers and gave him away in the end. Perhaps this is not the end of this mysterious plastic surgeon.

I approach the story wanting to start in peril. The reader is thrust in the middle of a strange and dangerous situation right away. Even the character is not sure of what is going on. This gives me the chance to explain it to them during the course of the action. It is also a way to introduce the characters in a less obvious way. I kept in mind that this was a short story collection, after all. The Purple Scar didn't need to be reintroduced with all his back story explored in each story. The reader would be like, "I know, I know!" Then, I want a break before the next action scene. I set up the backstory and introduce characters the reader would be seeing again. After that, it was time to advance the story with some action, and to show off some of the skills of our protagonist. I also want to show how they work well as a team so that when I split them up, it would cause some tension. Then, one by one, I split them apart and put them into situations without any help… or without any obvious help. Then, I set a cliffhanger and change the scene. After the solo fun, I sew the scenes back together and bring the group into a situation where they need each other. This is a Purple Scar story, though, and the Purple Scar needs to save the day. Sure, the other characters play their part, but even Miles Murdock is an extra to the Purple Scar. The reader has seen what drives him, and now they get to see him driven. We also see that he is not just driven by past misfortune. He cares for the safety of Dale and of what is right. He also needs to be careful not to become too zealous and dark. His friends help him with that too.

I strive for moments of light-heartedness. I enjoy characters who can be funny and have fun even when doing something dangerous. The ending needed to be light so the characters and the readers could have a final sigh and a smile. Ultimately, I want to stress the adventure side of the story over the science fiction/fantasy/horror/crime side. All of these can play a part in pulp, but in it's funnest form, it's adventure.

DAVID NOE -This is my bio and I'm sticking to it. I've been writing for several years now. I publish TYPO Magazine, a monthly magazine of fiction, poetry and occasionally, etc. (facebook.com/typomagazine1). I have several books available on Amazon (amazon.com/David-Noe/e/B00YNQZVAQ/). I like to write different styles and genres. Please check them out and leave a review. I also do comic book scripting. I've got some stories accepted and upcoming from Charlton Neo, Empire Comics and Pix-C. Find out all about my new stuff at facebook.com/tradeofthetricks.

HORROR HAS A NEW FACE

From the pages of the classic pulps comes the most frightening avenger of them all, the Purple Scar!

The handsome, debonair Dr. Miles Murdoch was a world famous plastic surgeon. His life was the stuff of dreams until it all turned into a heart-wrenching nightmare. Murdoch's brother, a dedicated police officer, is brutally gunned down while on patrol. Before dumping his body into the river, his murderers pour acid over his face as a final act of contempt. When the body washes ashore days later, Officer Murdoch's face is beyond recognition, a scarred, purple visage unlike any horror ever imagined.

It is the sight of this death grimace that transforms Miles Murdoch into an avenging angel. Vowing to bring justice to those responsible, the skilled surgeon molds a pliable rubber mask from that repulsive, mutilated face; a mask he dons to become the Purple Scar, the scourge of crooks and villains everywhere. He has become the physical embodiment of their worst fears brought to fiendish life.

Airship 27 now presents four brand new adventures of the creepiest pulp hero of them all, *the Purple Scar!*

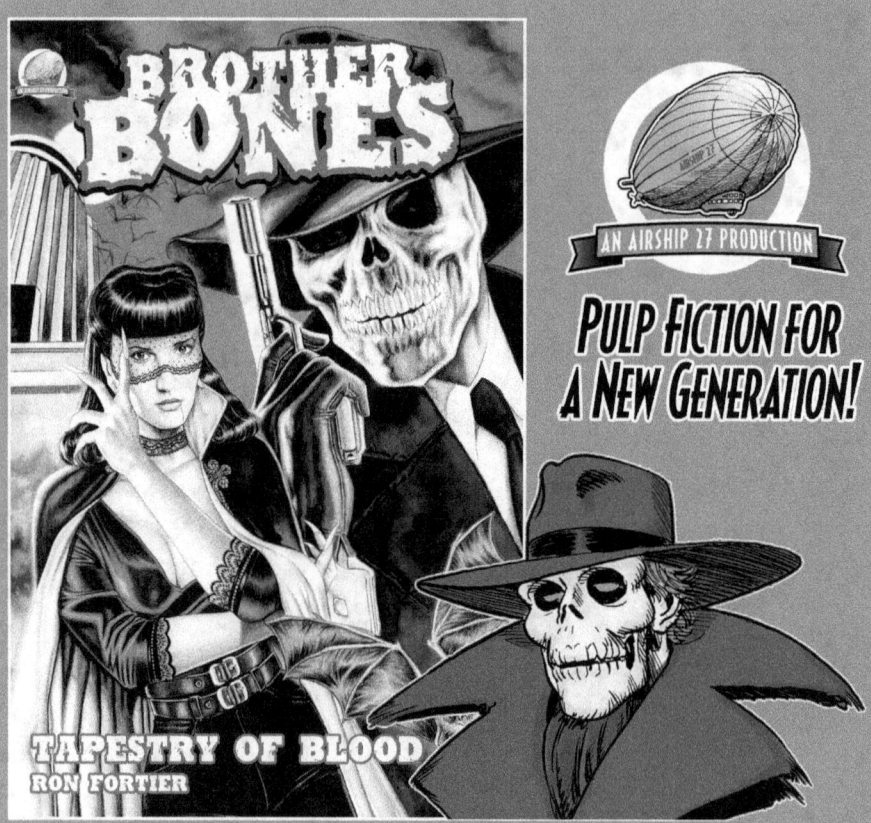

TAPESTRY OF BLOOD
RON FORTIER

WELCOME TO CAPE NOIRE

Located on the Northwest Coast, Cape Noire is a booming economic giant whose inner core has been corrupted by all manner of evil. From the sadistic mob bosses who ruthlessly control vast criminal empires to the fiendish creatures that haunt its maze of back alleys, Cape Noire is a modern Babylon of sin and depravity.

Amidst this den of iniquity strides a macabre warrior committed to avenging the innocent and holding back the tide of villainy. He is *Brother Bones, the Undead Avenger* and there is no other like him. A one-time heartless killer, he is now the spirit of vengeance trapped in an undying body. He is the unrelenting sword of justice as meted out by his twin .45 automatics

His face, hidden forever behind an ivory white skull mask, is the entrance to madness for those unfortunate enough to behold it. This new collection features five suspenseful, fast-paced, action-packed stories featuring pulp fiction's most original hero, Brother Bones. Time to draw the shades, light the candles and enter into a Tapestry of Blood!

FOR AVAILABILITY OF THIS AND OTHER FINE PUBLICATIONS CHECK THE WEBSITE: AIRSHIP27HANGAR.COM

www.ingramcontent.com/pod-product-compliance
Lightning Source LLC
Chambersburg PA
CBHW071240250626
47163CB00001B/261